PAYBACK IN PAXTON PARK

A PAXTON PARK MYSTERY BOOK 4

J. A. WHITING

To hear about new books and book sales, please sign up for my mailing list at:

www.jawhitingbooks.com

 Created with Vellum

For my family with love

1

_____

With the early morning sun rising over the mountain behind her, Shelly Taylor skied with care over the white powder of the resort's intermediate trails. Her friend, Juliet, stayed close by to offer encouragement and praise as the two made their way to the bottom for the third time that morning.

As employees of the resort, the young women were allowed to ski from 6am to 7am at no charge and this was the first time twenty-eight-year old Shelly had the courage to attempt the slopes since the car accident a year ago that took her twin sister's life and left Shelly with a long and painful recovery.

"You did great." Juliet high-fived her friend. "You were awesome."

"Yes, if you like skiing with someone who moves like an old lady." Shelly shook her head, but the excitement and joy of shushing down the slopes was written all over her wind-chilled face.

"It was the first time you've skied in over a year. You should be really proud of yourself." Juliet gave Shelly a warm pat on her back. "*I'm* proud of you. How is your leg doing?"

"I feel good, but it's probably due to the endorphins flooding my body from the thrill of skiing. In an hour or so, I probably won't be able to walk."

Juliet chuckled. "But it will have been worth it." Checking her watch, she asked, "Do we have time for another run?"

"I don't think I dare do another one," Shelly said. "I don't want to push it. Wait until I tell Jack I skied today. He'll be so excited." Jack and Shelly had been dating for about six months and both enjoyed the outdoor activities offered from living near the mountain and forest.

At the base of the hill to the right, a good-sized lodge, called the *barn* by the workers, was tucked into the trees where the slope's groomers and resort maintenance workers made their offices. The lodge-like building stood in front of several huge garages where snow equipment and trucks were kept.

Passing by on the way to the resort's main lodge, Shelly noticed the barn's front door was open. It was freezing outside. Why didn't someone shut the door?

A blood-curdling scream shot through the air and caused the two young women to halt in their tracks.

"What was that?" Juliet's gaze was pinned on the worker's lodge.

After exchanging glances, Juliet and Shelly skied towards the barn, and as they approached, a man raced out through the open door, bent over at the waist, and got sick onto the snow.

Unsnapping her skis, Juliet dropped her ski poles and ran to the man who they recognized as Troy Broadmoor, a resort employee and manager of the barn.

"What's happened?" Juliet put her arm over the man's shoulders and when he straightened up, his face was ghostly white.

"Are you okay, Troy?" Shelly glanced around trying to figure out why the man had screamed.

Troy, in his early thirties with sandy-colored hair and big brown eyes, looked from Juliet to Shelly like he had never seen another human being before. Wearing jeans and a long-sleeved, flannel shirt, the man blinked at them without speaking as his shoulders began to shake.

"Troy?" Juliet asked. "What's wrong? Are you ill?"

"No." Troy's eyes were wide and wild as he looked back to the building and gestured towards it. "Inside. Grant and Benny are inside. It's Grant and Benny."

"Are they working in the lodge?" Juliet questioned. When Troy didn't answer, she asked with a hesitant voice, "Is something wrong with them?"

Troy's pale face turned to Juliet. "Dead."

Hearing the word, Shelly felt like she'd been slapped and she took two fast steps back from Troy. "*Dead*? Are you sure? What happened to them?" A flood of anxiety shot through her body.

"Inside," Troy said as he shook his head from side-to-side. He'd been good friends with the two men and his pain from what he'd discovered was almost tangible. "Don't go in there."

Shelly stepped to the opened doorway of the building and peered gingerly into the first room to see nothing out of the ordinary ... chairs, desks with folders and papers resting on the tops, a lamp on each desk, and eight metal floor cabinets standing against one wall. "Where are they, Troy? Where are Grant and Benny?"

"Office." The sandy-haired man dropped to his knees in the snow, muttering and waving his hand in the air, so Juliet put her hand on his back to comfort him and then exchanged worried looks with her friend.

"I'm heading inside to see what's going on," Shelly said.

"Should you? Maybe stay out here. I'll call for help." Juliet used her free hand to unzip the pocket of her jacket and remove her phone.

Shelly peeked in through the door and raised her voice. "Hello? Grant? Benny? Is anyone inside?"

No response.

"I'm going to walk around the building." Shelly headed off to look in through the windows.

The sun's glare hit the front window's pane of glass making it impossible to see into the room so Shelly moved around to the rear of the lodge where she spotted one of the slope grooming machines parked off to the side by one of the equipment buildings.

Peering through the window into the manager's office, Shelly almost fell back onto her butt from the shock of what she saw.

Two men lay face down on the floor, pools of blood surrounding their bodies.

Shelly's stomach lurched and she sucked in several breaths of the icy cold morning air before running, as best she could in her ski boots, back to the front entrance.

"Grant. Benny." Shelly locked eyes with Juliet and shook her head. "I'm going inside to see if they might be unconscious."

Walking through the barn's main room, Shelly turned to the right into the hallway and moved past two doors to the office where the fallen men lay on the scuffed tiled floor. Being careful not to step in the blood, Shelly called their names even though she knew they both must be dead. Crouching next to Grant, she reached out her hand, but froze with it in mid-air, unable to touch him.

Don't touch. Don't disturb the scene.

With a racing heart and perspiration running down her back, the young woman watched the men's backs for a rise and fall that would indicate they were still breathing. The part of Benny's face that Shelly could see looked white and rubbery and her spirits fell as any hope the men were still alive slipped away. In slow motion, Shelly stood and looked around the room.

A chair had toppled over.

A few pieces of paper had fallen to the floor from the desktop.

A piece of something was on the floor beside the desk. A chunk of cement?

Feeling numb, Shelly shuffled across the cramped room to the opened closet and her jaw dropped. The big, black safe had almost been pulled from the floor. It had large, heavy bolts that attached it to the floor, but some had been chiseled out and removed. *How long had it taken someone to cut that safe out? Benny and Grant were killed because of a robbery?*

"Shelly, come out of there." Juliet called nervously from outside and the words broke Shelly out of her state of horror and disbelief, and she stumbled out of the building.

"What did you see?" Juliet asked as she turned away from Troy so he wouldn't hear their conversation.

"They're dead," Shelly whispered, her eyes glazed over.

"Are you sure? Is anyone else inside?"

"I didn't see anyone ... just Grant and Benny." Shelly sank down and sat in the snow away from Troy, all of her energy drained away.

"Could you tell what happened to them? Were they ... stabbed?"

"I don't think they were stabbed," Shelly mumbled. "I think they were shot."

Jayne Landers-Smyth, "Jay" for short, a long-time police officer with the town of Paxton Park and Juliet's older sister, jogged around the resort lodge with another officer and two EMTs and headed up the hill. Puffing as she approached, Jay asked, "What's happened in there?"

Juliet pointed to the door. "Two employees are in the office off the hall. We think they're both dead."

With their hands on their weapons, the officers entered the cabin and did a search, then called the all-clear so that the emergency medical workers could enter the building, and after fifteen minutes more, Jay emerged.

"The office safe was nearly stolen. The resort workers must have come in and disturbed the robbers as they were trying to remove the safe. Benny and Grant were shot and killed."

Juliet winced and tears filled her eyes. "Who would do this? Kill two guys just to steal a safe?"

"I can't say anymore," Jay told her sister.

When an EMT came outside to tend to Troy, Jay spoke gently to Shelly and helped her to her feet. The two went into the front space of the building where Jay asked the young woman for a statement about what had happened.

"I saw them through the window," Shelly said flatly. "Grant and Benny. I knew them ... not very well, but a group of us got together once in a while. The guys were in the group." Shelly made eye contact with Jay. "Why would someone kill them? Over the contents of a safe? How much money was in there? I'm not a police officer, but it looked like they were shot at close range, execution-style. Were the people who did this professionals?"

As a law enforcement officer, Jay was unable to confirm or deny Shelly's comments or answer her question about the contents of the safe, but the woman's eyes clouded over and she let out a long sigh.

2

Sitting at the kitchen table of Shelly's rented bungalow, the young women stared at their coffee mugs, stunned into silence. Shelly's Calico cat, Justice, perched on her owner's lap sensing her mood and trying to comfort her.

"I have to be at the bakery in an hour," Shelly sighed. "I don't know how I'm going to get any work done. I feel like all my energy has been sapped."

"I have to lead a cross-country ski tour this afternoon," Juliet said. "I wish they'd cancel all the planned activities today. All anyone will be asking me about will be the murders. What will I say?"

"Management will call a meeting," Shelly reassured her friend. "They won't cancel anything, but they'll give you ways to deal with the barrage of questions and comments you'll be getting. At least I work in the kitchen. I don't have to handle the tourists and guests."

Juliet leaned across the table and asked softly, "What do you think happened?"

"Grant and Benny got caught in the middle of a robbery," Shelly said with a sad shake of her head.

Looking pointedly at Shelly, Juliet asked another question. "Have you had any dreams recently?"

Caught off-guard in mid-swallow, the coffee caused Shelly to choke for a moment and the coughing motion jostled the cat in her lap. Swallowing hard to clear the last bit of liquid from her throat and dabbing at her watering eyes with her napkin, she took a deep breath. "No dreams."

"Nothing? Nothing that foreshadowed the robbery?"

Shelly shifted around uncomfortably. "I can't foresee things, you know. I can't tell the future. I just have dreams ... dreams that are probably the result of my sleeping mind working on things I've heard or experienced or thought about during the day."

Juliet tilted her head to the side and said with a soft tone of voice, "I think your dreams are a little more than that."

Since her twin sister, Lauren, died in the car accident, Shelly had been experiencing dreams where Lauren visited her and seemed to provide clues or information about Paxton Park crimes. Initially, Shelly had brushed off the suggestion that the dreams might be the result of a heightened perception of situations and people and the dreams might be her subconscious working on a problem while she slept.

In her police work, Jay had been employed in departments that occasionally used the help of a psychic and she kept an open mind about *specialized* skills. She explained to Shelly that her sleeping mind might be leading her to something she'd only noticed in passing during the day. The importance of those things might be highlighted in the dreams by Lauren's appearance. Shelly's subconscious might be pointing her to things overlooked while awake.

Jay invited Shelly to be an as-needed consultant to the police department and her duties included sitting-in on interviews, speaking with people, and offering her perspective in on-going investigations. Shelly believed she wouldn't be of any use, but if Jay thought her input was helpful, she felt she had a duty to assist in any way possible.

"Jay will ask you to help on this," Juliet said. "You

were familiar with Grant and Benny. You might notice things other people overlook."

"I know." A shudder ran over Shelly's shoulders. "I wish I understood these dreams. I wish I knew how to control them. I wish I wasn't so clueless about the whole thing. It seems like silliness to think my dead sister comes to me in dreams to help us solve a crime."

A tiny smile crossed Juliet's face. "But, she *has* helped on three recent crimes. Whether Lauren is really there in spirit pointing you to clues or your mind uses Lauren to highlight something important, it works. You can't discount your ... *gift*."

Shelly sighed inwardly and asked herself, *Is it a gift or a burden?*

LATE IN THE AFTERNOON, Shelly and Juliet sat in front of Jay's beat up old desk in her cramped office of the Paxton Park police station. Tapping at her laptop, Jay asked without looking up, "So what can you tell me about the three men?"

Juliet said, "Troy Broadmoor works as a scheduler and office manager for the mountain operations. He's always friendly, a nice guy, kind of serious."

Jay put her elbows on the desk and folded her arms. "Troy told me he overslept. That he was supposed to report to work at 5:30am, but didn't arrive until nearly 7am." An eyebrow went up on the police officer's face. "Coincidence?"

"It's possible, isn't it?" Juliet asked.

"Do you think he's lying?" Shelly questioned, her blue eyes pinned on Jay.

"I need to consider all the options," Jay told them. "Has Troy ever been late to work in the past? If not, why today? If he's late on occasion, then his tardiness this morning isn't a first-time thing and wouldn't be thought of as unusual."

"I don't know if he's ever been late," Juliet told her sister. "We only know him casually. We don't work with him."

"You're thinking if he was late to work today, it could be because he was in on the robbery?" Shelly asked.

"It crossed my mind," Jay said. Forty-three-year-old Jay was fifteen years older than her sister and was a twenty-year veteran of the Paxton Park police force. A tall, stocky woman, Jay had a keen intelligence, a calm, kind manner, and the ability to diffuse difficult situations. The officer was a well-respected and valued member of the community. "What do you know about Grant Norris and Benny Little?"

Juliet said, "They worked grooming the mountain, doing maintenance on the equipment, making sure the lifts were safe and in good working order, things like that."

"They told me they'd both worked at the resort for a number of years," Shelly said.

"Grant was married," Juliet said. "Benny had a live-in girlfriend. They seemed like normal guys, hard-working, enjoyed the outdoors, liked their jobs."

"When a group of us would go out for drinks or get together for some activity, Grant and Benny often joined in," Shelly said. "We'd all been out snow-shoeing together a couple of weeks ago."

"Did they seem like their normal selves?" Jay asked.

"I didn't notice anything out of the ordinary," Juliet said.

"I didn't notice anything either. Things seemed normal, but I was with Jack and a couple of other friends for the most part," Shelly said. Something had been picking at her since she'd been inside the maintenance building. "What was in that safe that was so important that it caused two men to lose their lives?"

Jay fiddled with a pen on top of her desk. "Seventy-five thousand dollars."

"Why was there so much money in there?" Juliet asked with wide eyes. "Don't they clear it out every day?"

"Why do they have any cash in the safe at all?" Shelly questioned. "What do they need so much cash for? They do maintenance. They aren't selling things."

Jay clarified, "The equipment is expensive, and expensive to maintain. The office manager has to make payments for gas and oil and parts and service when the resort employees can't fix things or when there's a warranty on a piece of equipment and it can only be serviced by a qualified, certified technician. Cash goes in the safe, checks are written, the money is sent to the bank ... it's all part of the resort's accounting procedures."

"Why wasn't the money taken to the bank?" Shelly asked. "They don't usually keep so much cash in the safe, do they?"

"It seems on certain days they do," Jay said. "Cash is removed and carried to the bank on Monday, Wednesday, and Friday afternoons."

"So it builds up over the weekend?" Juliet asked.

"Monday morning would be a good time to hit the safe then," Shelly observed.

Jay looked glum. "No one took the money to the bank last Friday afternoon. The person who does the pickups was out sick on Friday so there were cash deposits from several days in the safe."

"And somebody knew this," Shelly said.

"It seems so." Jay pushed at a lock of her short hair. "Who was it? Who shared this information with the thieves? Troy Broadmoor?"

"Oh, gosh," Juliet shook her head. "I can't see Troy being in on a heist."

"Maybe he wasn't in on the robbery," Shelly said thoughtfully. "Maybe he just spilled the beans in front of the wrong person."

"That could be," Jay said.

Shelly made eye contact with Jay. "Was there anything else in the safe besides money?"

Jay cocked her head to the side. "That's a good question."

"Who has access to the safe?" Shelly asked.

Jay said, "Troy. The usual pick-up person, Shannon Flay. She was the one who went home sick on Friday and was out on Monday. There could be others who had access. We'll look into it further."

A knock on the door jamb caused the three women's heads to turn.

Detective Andrew Walton, tall, slim, with sandy-colored hair, stood casually leaning his shoulder against the door, a little smirk on his face. "Having a pow-wow?"

"That's right," Jay's expression changed to one of annoyance. "What do you need, Andrew?"

The detective said, "I'm going out to the resort to talk with the director. Want to come along?"

"Give me five minutes. I'll meet you in the lobby," Jay said.

When the detective had disappeared down the hall, Juliet said, "Why is he so annoying? I can't even put my finger on why I don't like him."

"He's rude," Shelly said, "sort of arrogant and dismissive. He questioned me about an investigation a few months ago. I didn't care for his interviewing techniques. He made me feel guilty and on-edge."

"Andrew is a very effective law enforcement officer, but I sometimes have issues with his manner." Jay shook her head. "His cousin, Porter, recently transferred to the department here. He has a good reputation as an officer. He seems to be a very different person than the detective ... thankfully."

"Tell Detective Walton to keep his nose out of this investigation," Juliet sniffed.

"I'd love to, but it's not my place." Jay gave a shrug of her shoulder. "Anyway, he's the least of our worries."

3

Shelly rolled out the dough on the marble counter while reporting to Henry and Melody, the couple who ran the resort diner, about the early morning mystery she and Juliet stumbled on just a few hours ago.

Melody, in her sixties, petite, with silver-white hair cut short, made little gasping noises and kept lifting her hand to her face throughout the story. "What is going wrong with the world? So much trouble here in our little town."

"Paxton Park isn't really little, hon," Henry said gently, "what with all the tourists and visitors who come here. But our town is a microcosm of what's going on in the big cities. Too much crime. Too much hurt. Too much need and not enough help."

"Did you talk to Jay?" Melody asked. "Does she know who killed Benny and Grant?"

"Jay doesn't know yet. She's gathering information." Shelly used a reassuring tone despite feeling stressed and anxious over the murders. "The investigation has only just begun, but Jay has a good record of solving the toughest kinds of cases. We'll have to be patient and let the police do their work."

"Oh, my." With wide eyes, Melody shook her head. "It's downright frightening. The killer is out there walking around. He could come in here and place an order and we wouldn't even know he was the murderer. We'd cook his breakfast and speak pleasantly to him and off he'd go with a full tummy and a heart full of death." The older woman moaned. "Why would anyone break into the maintenance office?"

"There was money in the safe," Shelly said.

"Money. Was it a lot of money?"

"A good amount," Shelly told her.

"How would anyone know there was money in there?" Henry asked. "I wouldn't think to rob the maintenance building. I wouldn't think there was any reason to attempt it."

"You think it might have been an inside job?"

Shelly asked as she lifted the pie crust and placed it into the glass dish.

"It seems like there would need to be someone on the inside to coordinate the plan," Henry said. "To organize it all, to keep track of which employee is where, and when he or she is there so they could arrange the best time to hit the maintenance building."

"It makes sense," Melody said. "The thieves would need to know the best times of the day and week to hit the safe. How would someone who doesn't work at the resort know when the safe was vulnerable?"

"Someone who works there might have a big mouth and he might shoot it off no matter who is around." Shelly mixed the filling ingredients together. "Maybe the person needs to feel important so he reveals information that should be closely guarded."

"Information about when there were fewer people around must have been gathered by the killers." Melody filled the napkin holders. "No one was around this morning except Benny and Grant?"

"It seems not. Benny and Grant must have interrupted the robber's plans to chisel the safe out of the floor and make off with it," Melody said.

"I bet you're right," Shelly mixed some fresh lemon juice into the filling. "The robbers must have arrived early in the morning to steal the safe. They may have expected Troy to be in the office already and had plans to deal with him. Luckily for Troy, he overslept and didn't get in to work at his usual time. The place was empty when the robbers began to chisel, but soon Benny and Grant arrived after the slope maintenance truck conked out. They must have walked into the office looking for Troy to pick up a requisition slip to get the slope maintenance machine repaired."

"But instead of finding Troy, Benny and Grant discovered the robber trying to remove the safe from the office," Shelly said as she placed the top crust over the fruit filling and crimped the edges.

"It was not one of their lucky days," Henry grunted in disgust at the loss of two human beings' lives. "I'm sorry you had to see those bodies."

"I'm shaken up about it, but I'll be okay," Shelly said. "Did you know the men?"

"They came in from time to time for a meal," Melody's eyes grew sad. "Sometimes Grant and his wife, Emmy, came in together. We only knew them to exchange pleasantries with."

"You knew the guys?" Henry asked carefully.

"Only casually," Shelly explained.

Melody carried over a clean cookie sheet and placed it on Shelly's work table. "I was never that keen on Grant."

Shelly turned her eyes to the woman. "Why not?"

Letting out a breath, Melody said, "He seemed gruff, sort of self-absorbed. I didn't think he treated his wife very well."

Shelly was about to put the pie in the oven, but paused to ask, "What did he do that made you think that?"

"I don't know exactly." Melody gave a shrug. "He seemed … disinterested in her."

"Was that something new? Did you notice it before or just recently?" Something about Melody's observation piqued Shelly's interest.

"They didn't come in together very often. I can't say if his behavior towards his wife was new or not, but I noticed it when they came in for breakfast not long ago."

"When was it? Do you remember?" Shelly asked.

"Hmm." Melody tapped her chin with her index finger. "A week or two ago?"

"His wife's name is Emmy, right?"

"That's right. I know her mother. I don't know Emmy well." Melody carried some plates out to the dining room while Henry manned the grill for the lunch rush.

While her companions were busy, Shelly quietly worked on the list of bakery goods she was asked to make … some cookies, three lemon poppy seed loaves, and a chocolate layer cake, along with a cinnamon roll, and as she worked, her mind kept jumping back to the early morning scene of the dead men on the floor of the barn's office.

Was seventy-five thousand dollars enough to commit murder over? Apparently for some people it was. Shelly's heart sank with sadness.

WHEN HER WORK day was over, Shelly's boyfriend, Jack Graham, met her as she was exiting the diner and he wrapped her in a tight hug. "I'm so sorry about this morning. How are you doing?"

Jack was an adventure guide and ski instructor at the mountain resort and had returned to Paxton Park two hours ago from a three-day camping trip with a group of clients.

"I'm doing okay, I guess." Shelly held tight to the tall outdoorsman. "The crime scene keeps popping into my head. It was a terrible shock to see it."

The two walked arm-in-arm along the sidewalk.

"Should you talk to someone? A counselor? To help you deal with it?" Jack asked with concern.

"I'll be okay." Shelly squeezed the man's arm. "I have you and Juliet to talk with."

"How are you getting home?" Jack asked. Shelly didn't own a car. Since the accident, whenever she had to ride in a vehicle, anxiety would nearly smother her so she avoided passenger cars as much as possible and rode her bike when the weather allowed.

"I was going to walk."

Jack took her hand in his. "Then I'll walk with you."

Shelly told her boyfriend about the morning skiing and how happy she'd felt after doing several runs down the mountain. "We were only on the intermediate trails, but it was great. My leg was sore afterwards, but it was manageable." Shelly retained a limp in one leg from the accident and there was pain from time to time, but she'd been able to return to jogging and biking, taking it slow to build up her strength and stamina.

"When we finished the last run, Juliet and I were near the maintenance building down near the trees." Shelly took in a long breath and told Jack the rest of the story about the morning.

"I didn't know so much money was kept in the safe," Jack said. "I wonder how the robber knew it was there."

"That's the million-dollar question," Shelly said. "I'm thinking it couldn't have been random. The robber tried to chisel the safe out of the floor. He must have brought tools to do it. I can't imagine someone doing all that work without having a good idea about what was inside."

"So the thief had to have been given that information."

"And the safe must be heavy," Shelly noted. "I think there had to be two robbers. Two people would get the chiseling done faster and two would be needed to haul the safe out of the building."

Jack said, "They had to have a car or a truck to put the safe in. I'm sure Jay will look into whether someone noticed a vehicle outside the building early in the morning."

Shelly's face clouded. "I walked around the building this morning. Juliet and I must have been there shortly after the robbery took place. I didn't notice any tracks in the snow close to the building."

"You had something else on your mind at the time," Jack told her. "It would be easy to miss a truck's tracks when you were trying to determine where Grant and Benny were ... and if they were hurt."

"I should have been more aware."

"That's asking a lot under the circumstances. You're not a police officer."

When the wind kicked up, Shelly pulled a knitted hat out of her jacket pocket and slipped it onto her head against the biting cold. "How well did you know Benny and Grant?"

"Not well," Jack said. "We'd talk when we ran into one another or when we all went out in a group, but I was usually with you or one of my good friends so I never interacted with them all that much. To be honest, I wasn't that surprised to hear they were caught up in today's tragedy."

Shelly gave her boyfriend a questioning look. "Why weren't you?"

"There was something about those two. I can't put my finger on it. They were two guys I didn't take the time to get to know because, well ... they didn't seem like my kind of friends."

Shelly made eye contact with Jack trying to understand what he meant.

Jack shrugged. "Those two gave me the impression it wouldn't be hard for them to get into trouble."

4

The delicious odor of garlic bread and simmering spaghetti sauce tickled Shelly's nose as she entered the kitchen to find Jack using a wooden spoon to stir the sauce in the pan. Justice the cat sat in a chair watching the man work.

"My stomach is grumbling," Shelly tightened the belt of her fuzzy robe and gave her boyfriend a peck on the cheek. "I'm feeling better. A nice hot shower, a wonderful meal cooking on the stove, and oh, there is one more thing lifting my spirits. What is it?" she kidded. "Oh, now I know ... it's the handsome man standing in my kitchen cooking for me."

Jack smiled and reached his arm out to encircle

Shelly's waist. "I'm glad I make you happy ... or is it mostly the food that's making you feel better?"

"Hmm." Shelly tapped her finger against her cheek pretending to consider the question. "I'm not sure. I'll have to give it some thought."

Shelly poured glasses of red wine and lit candles while Jack plated their meals, and then they sat down to enjoy the pasta, salad, garlic bread, and each other's company.

The dinner was almost over when Shelly brought up the robbery. "I'm sorry to bring up the subject."

"Don't be sorry," Jack said sipping from his wine glass. "It's important to talk it out."

"Why did you say you wouldn't be surprised if Grant or Benny got mixed up with trouble?"

Jack said, "Neither one had ever done anything wrong that I know of, but I got the impression they could be risk-takers, always looking for a thrill. I could see them mixing in with unsavory characters, getting up to no good."

Shelly's eyes narrowed as she thought over what Jack had told her. "Do you think the robbery could have been an inside job? Do you think Grant or Benny or both of them might have had something to do with it?"

"It's a possibility." Jack rested his fork on his plate. "Would they have known how much money was in the safe?"

"I wouldn't think so, unless someone slipped and mentioned it," Shelly said. "Grant and Benny groomed the ski trails, did maintenance around the resort. They wouldn't need to know how much money was in the safe to do their jobs. They wouldn't have any reason to access it. That was handled by the office manager."

Jack's face was serious. "Troy Broadmoor."

Her boyfriend's meaning slowly dawned on Shelly and she asked with surprise, "You think Troy was in on it?"

"I don't think anyone can be discounted until the investigation gets going in earnest."

Shelly's shoulders dropped. "Wow. I never considered Troy could really be involved."

"He probably isn't, but he was at the building and he needs to be checked out."

"Troy was late for work this morning. He should have arrived an hour earlier. He said he overslept."

Jack's eyebrow raised. "Really? How convenient."

"Did he know the robbery was going to take place?" Shelly asked. "Is that why he didn't get to work on time? Was he staying clear of the place until he knew the robbers would be gone?" Shelly rested her chin in her hand. "I can't believe this."

"Right now, it's only speculation." Jack reached across the table for Shelly's hand. "But no one can be counted out until Jay has investigated them. Remember to be on guard if Jay asks you to talk to anyone. Don't give anyone a pass just because you know them."

"You're right. I have to be careful. I can't allow my judgment to be swayed because we're all resort employees." Shelly pushed her long brown hair over her shoulder. "If the men were killed by robbers who had no connection to the resort, how did those thieves find out how much money was in the safe? Or that there was a safe in the building?"

Jack took a moment to think about that. "What if they were outside contractors? They could have been hired to handle something the resort workers couldn't do or didn't have time for. They may have come and gone from the building. They could have seen Troy handling the money. They could have overheard something about the money."

When Justice jumped onto Jack's lap and purred, he chuckled. "The cat likes my ideas."

"I do, too," Shelly said. "They make a lot of sense."

"Has Jay asked you to help out?"

Giving a quick nod, Shelly said, "She asked me to go with her to speak with Grant's wife, Emmy, tomorrow. I am not looking forward to that. Just thinking about going to see that poor woman sends anxiety rushing through my veins."

"It'll be okay. Jay will do most of the talking," Jack said reassuringly.

Shelly fiddled with her napkin. "It seems like such an invasion of the woman's privacy. It seems like such an intrusion into her grief."

"It will be awkward, for sure, but Grant's wife will want his killer brought to justice," Jack said. "She'll be glad law enforcement is working hard to solve the case. She'll want to help any way she can."

"You're right," Shelly nodded as she stood to clear the dinner plates. "But I still don't want to go. I'm glad the meeting is not first thing in the morning." Putting the kettle on the burner for tea, Shelly removed some mugs from the cabinet and carried a platter of brownies to the table just as her phone buzzed with a text.

After reading the message and lifting her eyes to Jack, her expression was one of dread. "It's Jay. She wants me to go with her to see Troy Broadmoor."

"Tomorrow?"

With a sinking heart, Shelly shook her head. "Now."

Shelly went to her room to get dressed with Justice's green eyes watching her every move.

Jack hugged his girlfriend at the front door and warmed her heart with his words. "Justice and I will watch a movie. We'll be here waiting for you when you get back."

In the Broadmoor's living room, Jay and Shelly sat opposite Troy and his wife, Roberta. Troy was a mess. The rims of his eyes were bright red and the whites were bloodshot. The man was tall, athletic, and strong, but now looked shrunken as though he'd lost ten pounds since the morning. He'd always impressed Shelly as being capable and calm. Now he sat wringing his hands together as his eyes darted nervously around the room.

Roberta's face was drawn and worried watching her husband disintegrate right in front of her.

Although Jay had spoken with Troy earlier in the day, Roberta had called her in a panic at Troy's rapid downhill slide.

"Tell us how you're doing," Jay asked the man with a gentle tone.

Troy's gaze fell on Jay for a half-second before flicking away. "I'm okay." The voice was at half its normal volume and had a hoarse quality to it.

"Have you spoken with your doctor?" Jay asked.

"Not yet."

"He refused to go." Roberta gave her husband a worried look. "I thought Troy should have a chat with his doctor. The day has been awful. It's important to talk to someone. You can't handle something like this by being stoic."

"I can't believe they're dead," Troy whispered. "How did it happen? Why were they killed?" The man turned to Jay. "It was a robbery, wasn't it?"

"Yes. They attempted to steal the safe."

"Did Grant and Benny try to stop them? Is that what happened?"

"We're still looking into what happened," Jay assured him.

"I overslept," Troy muttered. "I didn't get to work on time. If I'd been there when I was supposed to be...." His voice trailed off.

"It's a good thing you weren't there. You might have been caught in the middle of it all." Jay chose her words carefully making sure not to say *you might have been killed, too.*

"Did you see anyone leaving the building when you arrived at work?" Shelly asked.

Troy's eyes were like lasers. "No."

"A car? Any kind of vehicle parked near the building?"

"No car. Nothing. At least, I didn't notice anything."

"Weren't the men supposed to be out grooming the trails at that time?" Shelly asked.

Jay said, "We believe Benny and Grant were having trouble with a piece of equipment and drove it back for maintenance. It was parked out back behind the building."

"I didn't notice it," Troy said. "I didn't see it."

"Did you hear anything when you went inside?" Shelly questioned. "Any noises? Did anything sound out of the ordinary?"

Troy's brow furrowed. "Sounds? No, nothing."

"Can you tell us again what happened when you went inside?" Jay asked.

Troy took in a long, deep breath. "I went inside. I headed for the break room to get a pot of coffee going. I'm usually the first one in, but I was late. It was ... quiet."

"Are other employees usually at work by the time you get there?" Shelly questioned.

"The maintenance guys are in first and they go out right away to take care of the slopes so they'll be ready when the park opens. Shannon is at her desk by that time, but she was out sick today. Mike comes in a little later."

"Mike?" Shelly asked.

"Maintenance and communication," Jay said.

"What does Shannon do?"

"She does accounts receivable and bookkeeping," Troy said.

Shelly made eye contact with Troy. "Did anything seem wrong this morning?"

"No," Troy used a forceful tone. "I didn't think anything was wrong. I made a cup of coffee and headed to my office." He stopped, cleared his throat. His breathing rate picked up.

Troy raised a shaky hand and then let it fall into his lap as a look of confusion washed over his face. "They were on the floor." The man stared at Jay and raised his voice as if that would alter the course of what happened early that day. "They were on the floor."

"Yes," Jay nodded slowly. "I'm very sorry."

"I didn't see anything," Troy returned to mutter-

39

ing, his voice barely above a whisper. "I didn't see anything."

Shelly watched the man closely. *Why did he keep saying that?*

5

Snowflakes drifted lazily down over the mountainside and the early morning light filtered through the evergreen trees. At any other time, Shelly would have marveled at the natural beauty, but not at that moment.

Walking from the resort's main building, around the side, and up the hill near the ski slopes, Shelly and Juliet trudged along behind Jay, Detective Andrew Walton, and his cousin, Officer Porter Walton, as the group headed for the maintenance offices. Yellow crime scene tape surrounded the barn and flapped whenever a breeze came up.

Andrew had been trying to banter with the young women, but Shelly and Juliet, feeling anxious and uncomfortable, gave him short replies and forced smiles.

"I'm still not clear why you two are joining us today," Andrew said.

"I explained the reason to you." Jay sounded long-suffering. "Which part of my explanation did you have trouble understanding?"

"Neither one of them is with law enforcement," Andrew said.

"Shelly is a hired consultant," Jay corrected. "And my sister is here to assist me by taking notes ... at no charge to the department."

"But they don't have any experience," Andrew persisted. He turned to the young women. "Do you?"

Before Shelly or Juliet could reply, Jay answered the question. "They have the necessary experience and have worked with me on previous cases."

Andrew chortled. "What are they? Psychics or something?"

Jay gave the man a death stare. "The five of us are working together here this morning. If you feel uncomfortable, you are free to ask for reassignment."

Porter walked along quietly, but he gave Shelly and Juliet an empathetic smile.

"So." Jay's eyes traveled over every inch of the

front of the building and after a few minutes, she lifted the yellow tape. "Shall we?"

Andrew unlocked the front door and pushed it open for everyone to enter. The heat had been turned down and the chill, empty air surrounded the group as they stepped inside.

Even though it wasn't really that cold in the main office space, Shelly couldn't help but shiver.

Juliet slipped off her gloves, pulled a tablet from her bag, and began taking notes.

"I'll run-through the timeline, as we know it right now." Jay lowered the zipper on her heavy, winter coat. "Benny and Grant arrived in the employee parking lot around the same time. They stopped to talk with another resort employee. That employee reported he saw the two men follow the walkway on their way up to the maintenance offices. The employee also reported the men were their usual talkative, cheerful selves. Their lunch containers were in the break room refrigerator so we know they came in here."

Jay walked slowly around the room while Andrew and Porter glanced at the items and papers on top of the desks. Shelly and Juliet stood near the entrance, watching and listening to Jay as she continued the story.

"Grant and Benny were seen on the slopes in the grooming vehicle doing what they do first thing every morning. The assumption is the machine was not working properly so the men returned to the maintenance area, parked it, and went inside the barn where the robbery was taking place. Troy Broadmoor was late that morning and the book-keeper was out sick."

"Lucky for them," Andrew noted. "Or we'd have *four* dead people on our hands."

"The other workers weren't scheduled to begin their shifts until thirty minutes to an hour after Troy discovered the bodies," Jay added. "The crime scene investigators were here all day yesterday and into the night. They'll be returning in about forty-five minutes. Let's look around in here and then go outside to walk the grounds. There are lots of foot-prints in the snow from yesterday's investigation, but I thought it would be helpful if we came this morning to have a little time without a horde of law enforcement personnel bumping into one another."

When everyone began moving through the building's various rooms, Porter sidled up to Shelly and Juliet.

"My cousin can be a little abrasive, but he's an excellent detective."

Shelly didn't want to share her views on Andrew with Porter so she gave the man a nod and moved into the kitchen-break room.

Juliet tapped at the screen of her tablet.

"You help your sister with administrative duties?" Porter asked.

"When she needs me, I step in, if I can. I work full-time for the resort as an adventure guide and instructor and my hours are irregular so sometimes I can help out."

"And the other woman, Shelly? She's a consultant?"

Juliet looked up from her notes. "She works as a baker for the resort on a part-time basis. She has some skills the police department finds useful so they ask her to step in on occasion."

"Has she worked previously in law enforcement?" Porter asked.

Juliet fibbed. "I don't know her work history."

"Is she ex-military?"

"I'm not sure of her background. Why not ask her?" Juliet smiled and moved away from the officer.

Walking slowly around the kitchen and break-room, Shelly ran her hand over the tabletop where the workers ate and gathered, and her fingers touched some tiny crumbs left behind from previous days.

She opened the refrigerator to see a carton of milk, a piece of cake wrapped in cellophane, some yogurt containers, and a couple of bottles of salad dressing.

A brown lunch bag sat on the fridge shelf with the word *Benny* scrawled on it. Shelly's heart squeezed. Before closing the door, she noticed a black metal lunch box shoved to the side and wondered if it belonged to Grant.

Reaching for it, she stopped when Juliet spoke to her from the entrance to the kitchen. "I'm going to Troy's office. Will you come with me?"

It was the last place Shelly wanted to see, but she gave a nod and closed the refrigerator door.

Andrew squatted down in the corner near the spot where the safe stood and he looked up briefly when he heard the young women's footsteps and then returned to photographing the now mutilated cement floor with his phone.

Shelly and Juliet stationed themselves by the door just inside the room and glanced around without advancing any further into the office. Their eyes were drawn to the blood that had dried in thin puddles on the floor.

The room seemed close and stifling and Shelly wanted to flee, but she stood still not wanting to appear unable to handle the investigation. Averting her gaze from the blood, she let her eyes roam around the room.

A metal toolbox was overturned on the tiles with some of the contents spilling out. Small chunks of cement littered the floor from the previous morning's chiseling and attempted removal of the safe, and Shelly noticed something shiny under the baseboard on the far wall. It looked like a coin had rolled there or maybe a nail from the toolbox had been kicked across the floor.

"What do you think happened?" Juliet addressed the question to Andrew. "Did the men hear a noise in here and came to see what was going on?"

Andrew leaned back on his heels. "That could be how the deceased ended up in here ... or the thief or thieves heard the men come into the building and went out to the main room to meet them. The guys were herded back here and...." The detective's voice trailed off and he shrugged. "Have you seen Porter?"

Juliet said, "He was in the main room with me for a bit. I haven't seen him for a while."

"I'll find him." Andrew stood and left the office and as soon as he was gone, Shelly let out a long breath, leaned against the wall, and closed her eyes. "I'm glad he's gone. I didn't want him to see how shook up I am."

"Are you okay?" Juliet gently touched her friend's arm. "Do you want to go outside?"

"I'll be fine. I just need a few seconds to collect myself. The images of the dead men on the floor in here keeps flashing through my mind. I wish I hadn't seen it."

"Come on." Juliet lightly tugged on Shelly's jacket. "Let's get out of here. We'll go outside and look around. I've had enough of this building."

As they passed the kitchen-breakroom, Shelly took a quick look inside and a strange feeling came over her causing her to quicken her pace to hurry after Juliet.

Stepping out into the cold, refreshing air, Shelly took several deep breaths and tried to relax her tensed muscles by stretching her arms out behind her. "I felt like a caged animal in there," she confided to her friend. "I'd like to go for a run or a long bike ride to let out my nervous energy."

"Maybe we can do something later in the day." Juliet glanced around for Jay.

Shelly pointed. "There are footprints in the new snow. She must be out back."

When they rounded the corner of the building, they spotted Jay standing at the edge of the fir trees.

"What are you looking at?" Juliet asked.

Jay didn't turn, only pointed between the evergreens. "One of the fire roads is right over there. Someone could have driven up and left a vehicle parked on the road."

"You think the robber came this way?" Shelly asked. "Approached the maintenance building through these trees?"

"It seems the smartest way to come at it. When they get here, I'll speak with the investigators about the road. I'd bet some money they're thinking the same thing I'm thinking."

"Maybe they spotted some tire marks," Shelly's tone was hopeful.

"We didn't have fresh snow the night before. There might have been multiple old tracks from vehicles, hikers, fat bikes. It will be hard to sort it all out," Jay said.

Looking down the hill towards the resort and then back to the work building, Shelly asked, "Are there security cameras anywhere?"

"There's one at the back of the building facing the small lot where the trail-groomers and snow removal vehicles are kept." Jay gestured in the direction of the camera. "The investigators took the tape last night. My guess is either the camera doesn't work or the images will show nothing. The robber doesn't strike me as a dummy. He wouldn't park in the lot and waltz over here like he's on holiday. This guy, or guys, they're smart."

"Great," Juliet groaned.

"We'll just have to be smarter," Jay said with conviction.

6

Thirty-year-old Emmy Norris had bleached blond, shoulder-length hair and the bluest eyes Shelly had ever seen. The woman was very slender, but she did not have the look of a runner or an athlete. The whites of her eyes were bloodshot and her grief made the muscles of her face look loose and rubbery. A small white dog sat on Emmy's lap and its dark round eyes scanned with interest the people sitting on the sofa across from her.

Jay did the introductions and expressed condolences to the woman.

Shelly and Emmy had met several times at some resort activities, but had never spoken at length.

Emmy squeezed a disintegrating tissue, swallowed hard, and nodded. "I don't know what I'm going to do without Grant's salary. I know it's a terrible thing to be thinking about, but I'm so worried about it. Between that and Grant being gone, I can't sleep at night. I toss and turn and cry and then toss and turn some more."

"Do you have family nearby?" Jay asked gently.

"No, but my sister is coming from New Jersey. She'll be here tomorrow." Emmy dabbed at her eyes.

Shelly sat on one side of Jay and Officer Porter Walton sat on the other.

Porter said, "Make an appointment with the resort's human resources department. They can review any benefits or compensation you might be due because of the loss of your husband."

"Oh, okay." Emmy blinked. Shelly wasn't sure if the woman would remember to contact human resources and hoped Jay would follow-up to make certain Emmy didn't forget.

"How was Grant lately?" Jay asked. "Did he seem like anything was bothering him?"

When Emmy took in a long breath, her lips trembled slightly. "He was his usual self. Nothing seemed wrong." Looking down at her hands, she said softly, "We had a little fight before he went to work yesterday. I feel really bad about it."

"What was it about?" Jay asked.

"Stupid things. Grant has a hard time doing things around the house. I have to nag him to get things done. I can't be the one who does it all. I've told him again and again. I work full-time, too." Emmy's expression was tinged with defensiveness.

"Of course," Jay said kindly. "If everyone pitches in, a household runs more smoothly."

Emmy sat up a little straighter. "That's right. That's what I mean. I told him so."

"Did you know Benny Little?" Jay asked.

"Sure. I knew him. Poor Benny." Emmy shook her head slowly.

"Did he and Grant get along?"

"They were pals."

"Did they socialize after work?"

"Sometimes they'd get a drink, watch a game on TV. Sometimes they'd get together with some of the other resort employees. I'd go once in a while, but not much. I don't like sports or outside activities."

"Was there anything bothering Grant?" Shelly asked. "Was he worried about anything?"

Emmy blinked fast a few times. "I don't think so."

Shelly asked a more specific question. "Did he say anything about work? Was anything going on at work that was bothering Grant?"

"No. Grant liked his job." Emmy ran her hand over the dog's fur.

"How long had you and your husband been married?" Jay asked.

"Ten years. We got married young."

"How would you describe the marriage?"

Emmy's large blue eyes got bigger. "What do you mean?"

"Was the marriage strong? Were you both happy in the marriage?" Jay asked.

Lifting one shoulder in a shrug, the woman said, "It was normal."

"Normal happy?" Jay asked.

"I guess so." Emmy leaned back a little. "We were married ten years. We dated for four years before that. You know. Things change."

"Was your husband faithful?"

"Yeah. Mostly." Emmy pushed at her thin bangs.

"Were you faithful to Grant?" Jay asked.

The woman's eyes flashed. "What's this stuff got to do with anything?"

Jay's face maintained a neutral expression and she kept an easy tone of voice. "We're trying to determine your husband's state of mind. If anything had upset him, if he was unhappy or angry or worried about something. If he might have had a disagreement or an argument with someone. If money was tight. Things that might cause stress. Things like that."

"Have you ever had an affair?" Officer Walton asked.

"No. Not an affair." Emmy's lips pursed.

"Did you see someone for a time?" Walton asked.

Emmy looked away and turned her gaze out of the living room window. "Once I did. I saw a guy for a couple of months, but then I ended it."

"Why did you decide to end it?" Walton questioned.

"I didn't really like him. He was sort of boring."

"Did Grant know you were seeing someone?" Jay asked.

"He knew." The corners of Emmy's mouth pulled downward. "Grant didn't care. He didn't want me to leave him, but he didn't care about a fling once in a while. Why would he? What was good for him, was good for me, too."

Shelly was slightly surprised by the woman's comments. When they first arrived at the small cottage tucked onto a piece of land at the base of the mountain, she'd expected a grieving wife who had lost her young husband. Emmy was grieving, but a good amount of her emotion seemed based on financial concerns, and not on the loss of someone she loved.

"So Grant occasionally engaged in a *fling*?" Shelly asked.

"Sure he did. You can ask that bookkeeper at the barn. Grant had the hots for her."

"Who do you mean?" Jay asked, but had a good idea who Emmy meant.

"That bookkeeper. Shannon. Shannon Flay." A pout formed on the woman's face.

"Were they seeing each other now?" Jay asked.

"I think they stopped about a month ago." Emmy raised the mangled tissue to dab at her eyes.

"Why did they stop seeing each other?" Officer Walton asked.

"Who knows? Maybe Grant got tired of her. We didn't talk about that kind of stuff."

"Did it bother you that your husband saw other women?" Walton asked.

"Once in a while it did."

"So you had an open relationship of sorts?" Jay asked.

Emmy exhaled. "Sort of."

"Did Grant end the relationship with Shannon or was she the one who decided to end it?" Shelly asked.

For a split second, a flash of anger, or maybe annoyance showed on the woman's face. "I have no idea. I told you Grant and I didn't talk about stuff like that."

Jay asked, "Can you tell us about yesterday morning? Was it a normal morning?"

Emmy blinked at the police officer. "A normal day. Yes. I got up first, showered, went to the kitchen for breakfast. Grant got up and showered. I made lunches. Grant came in and complained that we were out of his favorite cereal. I told him he could have picked some up on his way home the day before. Everything wasn't my job." Emmy sighed. "We bickered at each other until I left for work. Over nothing. Silly things. I feel bad that was the way it was the last time we were together." A tear rolled down her cheek.

When Emmy batted away the moisture on her face, Shelly asked, "What did Grant use to take his lunch to work?"

Emmy gave Shelly a look like she thought she was crazy. "You mean his lunch box?"

Shelly nodded. "What did it look like?"

Tilting her head to the side, she said, "Black metal. Kind of banged up. Why?"

"I saw a lunch box like that in the breakroom refrigerator. I wondered if it belonged to Grant."

Officer Walton leaned forward and looked at Shelly with an odd expression, but he didn't say anything.

"Did Grant have any enemies?" Jay asked.

"Enemies? There were some people he didn't like. Some people didn't like him."

"What caused the disagreements?"

"It was just guys being guys. Someone would make a comment and the other person would take offense," Emmy said.

"Did Grant get into physical fights with people?"

"When he was in his early twenties he did. Not much now."

Jay held her pen over the notebook page. "Did Grant mention anyone who was bothering him recently? Anyone he thought was a pain in some way?"

Emmy scrunched up her face in thought. "There was a guy at work. He's new. Grant said he was full of himself, acted like he knew everything. The guy didn't like to hear any suggestions about how to do things. Grant said he didn't like him."

"What was the man's name?" Shelly asked.

"Something starting with an F. Finny? I think that's it. Yeah."

"He works at the barn?" Walton asked.

"I think so," Emmy said. "Yeah, he does."

"Can you think of anything else we should know?" Jay asked.

"Will you catch who killed Grant and Benny?" Emmy's face hardened.

"We'll do everything we can to bring someone to justice for the killings," Walton said.

Emmy leaned down and put her cheek against her dog's soft fur. "I don't care about justice. I care that the killer dies in prison for what he did. Grant was no saint, but he didn't deserve that. He didn't deserve to die like that. He was gunned down like a dog. He was at work. He was doing his job. It's not right what happened. Grant and Benny woke up and went to work just like every other day. They got killed by some monster who was stealing the safe." Tears started to flow again and dropped onto the dog's back. "It just isn't right."

7

After leaving Grant and Emmy Norris's house, Shelly rode in the backseat of the police car with Jay driving and Porter Walton in the passenger seat.

Shelly could feel the anxiety gripping her stomach as Jay maneuvered the car through the twists and turns in the country road.

Looking into the rearview mirror into the backseat, Jay asked, "Are you okay, Shelly?"

Porter turned slightly to look behind. "Is something wrong?"

"Shelly gets car sick sometimes." Jay covered for the young woman's anxiety knowing she probably didn't want to get into a discussion about the accident that killed her sister and left Shelly with a limp and pain in her leg.

"Oh," Porter said. "Do we need to stop? Do you need some air?"

"I'm okay," Shelly said and decided to make conversation to distract her from the ride. "How is the office manager doing? He was pretty shaken up when we went to see him the other evening."

Jay said, "After we left the house, Troy's wife took him to the hospital. The doctor prescribed a tran-quilizer. He'll be out of work for a few weeks. Finding the bodies hit him hard."

"Was he good friends with Grant and Benny?" Shelly asked.

"Friendly was how he described it," Jay said.

"I hope the passing of time will help Troy better handle what happened." Shelly rubbed at her temples wishing she could exit the vehicle. She'd rather walk for miles than be trapped inside a car.

"What did you think of the interview with Grant's wife?" Porter asked.

"It wasn't what I was expecting," Shelly admitted. "I thought Emmy would be heartbroken over Grant. I guess she was in a way, just not the way I thought."

"She was honest though," Porter said. "Even though the marriage wasn't picture-perfect, she still seemed fond of Grant. She's worried about money. She might struggle without his paycheck, but she'll probably sue the resort so in the end, she might make out okay."

"They seemed to have an understanding with one another that worked for them," Jay said. "Neither one got too hung up when the other one was seeing someone else. The both ignored the other's indiscretions. Being married to each other was probably comfortable and convenient."

"Yeah," Porter said. "They could have their flings, but could use the fact they were married to keep the affairs casual and non-committal." The police officer turned his head a little and addressed Shelly. "Why did you ask Emmy about that lunch box?"

Shelly shrugged. "I saw it in the refrigerator. I was trying to imagine Grant and Benny's morning, what they did, where they were at what time. I was picturing their movements that morning so I asked if the lunchbox I saw belonged to Grant."

"Does it have some significance?" Porter asked.

"I guess not." Shelly clutched her hands together in her lap, counting the minutes until she got dropped off at her house.

"We'll be needing to talk with Shannon Flay," Jay

said. "From what Emmy said, Grant and Shannon were close, at least they were at one time."

"I wonder if Shannon owns a gun?" Porter asked.

Shelly's eyes widened. "Shannon? You think she may have killed the men?"

"The woman knew what was in the safe," Porter pointed out. "She may have held a grudge against Grant. Maybe she enlisted a friend to help her remove the safe and get rid of Grant. Benny was just collateral damage."

Shelly groaned.

"It's all possible," Jay said. "We'll have a chat with her."

"According to Emmy, Grant didn't get along with the new guy at work. What was his name?" Porter asked.

"Finny," Shelly replied.

"He'll need to be interviewed as well." Porter looked out the side window at the countryside. "It sure is pretty here. Much nicer than working in the city." The man snorted. "I thought a resort town might be boring, with not much investigatory work necessary. Guess I was wrong."

Jay traveled down the quaint main street of Paxton Park and made the turn onto Shelly's lane, stopping at her rented cottage.

"Pretty house," Porter remarked.

"Thanks." Shelly pushed the door open eager to get out, thanked Jay for the ride, told the law enforcement officers she'd see them soon, and then hurried to her front porch, little beads of sweat trickling down her back.

Juliet lived next door to Shelly and had been waiting for her to come home. When she heard the car door slam, she went outside to meet her friend. "How did it go?"

Shelly stopped before opening her door. "It was okay, but the car ride almost did me in. Want to come in while I change?"

Justice was waiting inside. She flicked her tail around and rubbed against the young women's legs and then followed Shelly into the bedroom and sat on the bed while her owner changed.

"Tell me about the interview." Juliet had made tea and set two mugs on the table while Shelly went over what had been said at the meeting with Emmy Norris.

"At least the conversation brought up two more people who need to be interviewed," Juliet said. "Grant and the bookkeeper had an affair, huh? Shannon Flay is going to have to be very upfront when she talks to police to avoid becoming a suspect."

"I feel like there's something we're missing." Shelly ran her finger over the rim of her cup.

"Like what?"

With a smile, Shelly said, "If I knew, I'd look into it."

"Is it a vague feeling or are you in a certain place or talking to someone in particular when the sensation strikes?" Juliet asked.

"Vague, I guess. I can't connect it to anyone or any place."

"If it's important, you'll figure it out," Juliet said encouragingly.

Shelly pushed back from the table. "I need a break. I've been looking forward to this all day."

"Let's go then."

THE TWO FRIENDS barreled down the trails on fat-tire bikes – the wide tires provided extra grip and traction and a wider contact surface on difficult terrain like snowy mountain trails allowing riders to travel over the paths in most any weather. Riding up the hills was harder, but for the two young women being outside under the snow-covered evergreens enjoying nature was worth the effort.

Once they reached the flatter section of the trails, Shelly and Juliet rode side-by-side.

"I needed that." Shelly's pink cheeks glowed from the exercise. "I love being able to bike in the winter. With the snow cover, everything is so quiet and peaceful."

"It's perfect," Juliet said. "I led a group over the trails this morning. They loved it. There are more tourists here this year than ever." She gave a smile and a chuckle. "Which means job security for me."

"All the activities the resort offers really brings in the guests. The skiing, sledding, toboggan course, skating, the tubing hill, these fat bikes. Everyone can find something fun to do here."

Juliet nodded. "Management has been smart about expanding the options. They've done a great job."

A breeze kicked up and shook some of the branches hanging over the trail sending snow off the pines down onto the young women's heads like a tiny avalanche. Getting pummeled by the snowfall caused the two to howl with laughter.

After brushing the snow from their bike helmets,

Juliet started off at a face pace. "Come on. Race you to the top."

Off they went, pedaling like maniacs.

Juliet took the corner fast and her bike skidded on some snow-covered ice, almost toppling before she was able to right it again.

Shelly watched her friend's gyrations and chuckled. "Nice save."

Pulling to the side of the trail, they stopped for a water break and to catch their breath. Despite the late afternoon sun shining between the pines, the air was crisp and cold and Shelly's lungs burned a little from breathing in the freezing air.

From their position on the trail, they could look down on the skiers as they made their way along the manicured slopes toward the main lodge of the resort. The colorful jackets and ski pants on the skiers looked festive against the white snow.

Juliet gestured past some bare branches. "You can see the barn from here."

A shiver ran down Shelly's back. "No one is working in there yet, are they?"

"The police are letting the employees back inside tomorrow. I bet they're not looking forward to that."

"I know I wouldn't be." Shelly scanned the building and the grounds with a sense of dread. "Did

Jay mention anything about the security tape the investigators took from the roof?"

Juliet frowned. "It was exactly as Jay said it would be."

"The camera wasn't working?"

"No, it worked. It just captured nothing. It was aimed at the lot where the equipment is parked and the robber didn't go anywhere near there."

"He must have known to avoid the lot," Shelly guessed. "He must have been aware there was a camera pointed in that direction."

"Or somebody told him about it," Juliet suggested.

"Why would the robber kill two men over the money in the safe? It wasn't a million dollars or anything."

"My guess is because Grant and Benny saw his face."

"No disguise?" Shelly asked. "If the thief knew there was a lot of money in the safe, then they would know what time the workers arrived. Troy Broadmoor overslept. He was supposed to be at work an hour before he actually arrived. Why wasn't the robber gone by then?"

"The chiseling must have taken longer than he thought. He probably felt he couldn't just abandon the safe. He'd done a lot of work to get it out. He must have been determined to finish the job."

"Would you carry a gun to steal a safe?" Shelly asked.

Juliet's forehead scrunched up. "What do you mean?"

"If you were only going to steal a safe from a building, would you bring a gun along? If you did, you must have had the idea you would have to shoot someone, right?"

"Unless the robber only wanted to use it to frighten someone who happened upon him."

"Why didn't he wear a disguise?" Shelly asked. "Why didn't he just run away? No. Instead, he shot two men in cold blood. It seems kind of desperate to me."

"Well, he was desperate. Desperate to steal the safe."

Shelly blew out a breath in disgust, and squinting her eyes, she said, "Someone's down there."

"Where?"

"By the back of the building." Shelly pointed. "In the trees. See? Someone's staring at the barn."

"I see him. Why is he watching the building?"

Juliet shaded her eyes from the glare of the sun's rays low in the sky. "Isn't that Porter Walton?"

"It *is* him," Shelly said. "I recognize his ski parka. What's he doing? Why is he in the woods staring at the barn?"

8
———

When Shelly and Juliet arrived at the quiet café at the edge of Paxton Park, they took a seat in a booth at the back of the place to wait for Benny Little's girlfriend to arrive.

Thirty-year-old Betsy Billings entered the establishment, spoke to the hostess, and then followed the woman leading the way to the back booth. Wearing jeans, boots, and an unzipped, blue ski parka, Betsy had long dark hair and a trim, athletic build.

A few people seated at tables noticed Betsy as she passed by, her eyes straight ahead, and they turned to their friends or spouses to whisper about the poor young woman whose boyfriend had been murdered.

Shelly and Juliet stood to introduce themselves and then Betsy slid onto the bench across from them and the three made some small talk to break the ice.

Jay had already interviewed Betsy, but she hoped Shelly and Juliet might uncover something additional if they spoke with her in casual surroundings.

"Thanks for meeting us," Shelly told the woman.

"I'm glad to talk to you if it can help find Benny's killer." Betsy almost winced as the words came out of her mouth and her voice was soft when she added, "I can't believe this has happened. It's a nightmare. Who would want to kill Benny?"

"How long had you and Benny been together?" Juliet asked after the waitress took their orders.

Betsy's shoulders slumped. "Two years." A few tears gathered in her eyes, but she blinked them away.

"How did you meet?" Juliet asked.

"It was a blind date set up by my friend. Her boyfriend knew Benny and thought we'd make a nice match." The edges of Betsy's lips turned up at the memory. "He was right. We were a good match."

"You were living together?" Shelly asked.

Betsy gave a nod. "We rented a small house. We'd lived there for almost a year. The lease is coming up for renewal. I don't want to stay. I'm going to move in with my sister. She lives on Cape Cod." The young woman reached into her pocket and removed a black velvet box. "I've been cleaning out the house, going through Benny's things and packing them up. I know it sounds like I'm uncaring doing that so soon, but I just can't take being there without him so I'm forcing myself to do it." She opened the box to reveal a sparkling diamond ring. "Benny had been hinting around about us getting married. I found this in his things." Betsy brushed at her eyes. "He never got to give it to me."

Shelly's heart tightened at the couple's lost future together. "I'm very sorry."

Stuffing the box back into her pocket, the young woman took off her jacket and placed it on the bench next to her. "Officer Landers-Smyth is your sister?" she asked Juliet.

"Yes." Juliet nodded. "Occasionally, Shelly and I work for the police department doing interviews or research for them. They're always short-handed and they have to work within budget constraints so we get brought in on a case-by-case basis as needed."

"Your sister was very nice to me," Betsy said. "It was hard to answer her questions. I'd just heard about what happened to Benny and I was a mess. She was very kind and understanding."

Juliet smiled. "That's my sister. I couldn't ask for better."

"I'm close to my sister, too," Betsy said. "We're lucky, I guess."

A wave of sorrow washed over Shelly from the talk of loving sisters, and wanting to turn the conversation to something else before Betsy could inquire whether she had a sibling, Shelly asked, "Had Benny seemed off lately? Was anything bothering him?"

Betsy's facial expression became serious. "I don't think so. He didn't bring anything up with me."

"Did he seem quieter than usual or maybe a little short-tempered?" Juliet asked.

Thinking over the question, Betsy's brow furrowed. "Things seemed normal."

"Any arguments with people at work? Was anyone bugging him or bothering him?" Shelly asked.

"Not that I know of. Benny hadn't complained about anything."

"There's a new guy at work?" Juliet asked. "Finny is his name?"

"Yeah." Betsy's brown eyes flashed as they lifted to Juliet's. "Does he have something to do with what happened to Benny?"

"No, no," Shelly said reassuringly. "We don't have any reason to suspect the man. We're only trying to establish relationships and connections between people. We're gathering information about the workers at the resort, friends, family members, associates."

"Did Benny get along with Finny?" Juliet asked.

"Sure. At least, I think so. Benny never said anything against him."

"We've heard that Grant didn't like Finny," Shelly said.

Betsy shrugged. "Grant could be fussy. He picked at things. He got annoyed with things. Some people look for reasons to get riled up. I told Benny he shouldn't get drawn into Grant's issues. Stay friendly with everyone, that's what I told him. Let things go. You don't want trouble at work. You want a nice working environment."

"Did Benny agree with you?" Shelly asked.

"Yeah, he did. Benny was easy-going. He wasn't looking for any drama. Do his work, get along with the others. That's what he was like."

"Did Benny like Grant?" Juliet asked.

"Sure, he did. They'd worked together for years. Benny knew how Grant was, but he wouldn't feed into Grant's complaining."

"What did Grant complain about?"

"Everything." Betsy rolled her eyes. "Grant was okay, but he had a lot of opinions. The pay wasn't good enough. The work was too demanding. Some people didn't pull their weight at the barn. Stuff like that. Benny and I thought it was best not to complain about everything. Otherwise, you'll just be miserable all the time."

Shelly nodded in agreement. "Did Benny ever worry about his safety at work?"

Betsy straightened up looking surprised. "His safety? No. He never mentioned anything like that."

The waitress delivered the food and the women ate in silence for a few minutes before Juliet asked the next question. "Do you know Shannon Flay?"

Before answering, Betsy took in a long breath. "I met her a few times."

"Did Benny get along with her?"

"Sure."

"Did he ever say anything about her job performance?"

"I don't remember him saying anything about her work."

"Did Benny ever say anything about Shannon's friendships at work?" Juliet asked.

Betsy leaned forward with a pointed expression. "Look, I know about Shannon. You don't need to dance around it. She liked to flirt. Sometimes, it was more than just flirting. She liked the guys and some of the guys liked her back."

"Not Benny though," Shelly said.

"No, not Benny." Betsy shook her head. "Benny was faithful. He didn't need a fling or an affair. He thought that kind of behavior was disrespectful to the person you were with. Benny was a good man."

"What about Grant?" Shelly asked.

"Grant wasn't like Benny in that way. I don't want to speak ill of the dead," Betsy said, "but Grant enjoyed women. He wasn't a faithful partner."

"Did he and Shannon...?"

A frown formed over Betsy's face. "Have you talked to Grant's wife?"

Juliet nodded.

"Then Emmy must have told you that Grant had been seeing Shannon. Emmy claimed she was fine with an open relationship, but I'm not so sure if she really felt that way or not."

"Grant and Shannon's affair was over before the break-in at the barn?" Shelly asked.

"I think so," Betsy said.

"Did Benny ever mention whether Grant or Shannon was bitter about the end of the affair?"

"I don't know the details." Betsy sighed. "Benny and I tried to stay out of other people's business."

Juliet rested her fork on her plate. "Do you have any guess as to what happened at the barn the other morning?"

Betsy's breathing rate increased and as her eyes flicked about the café, she placed her hand against her stomach. "I don't know. I don't have any idea. All I know is that Benny is dead." The young woman bowed her head. "My life is a mess. I never considered a future where Benny wasn't in it. We lived a simple life. We were good to each other. We loved nature ... skiing, hiking, kayaking. We took turns cooking dinner. I made his lunch for him every morning. He brought me flowers." A tear rolled down Betsy's cheek.

The woman's words sent a rush of anxiety prickling through Shelly's body.

"You have no idea what's it like to lose someone you love," Betsy said softly.

Shelly didn't say a word, but, yes, she knew very well what that was like.

WHEN THE INTERVIEW was over and Shelly and Juliet were walking through the café parking lot to the car, a vehicle rolled up beside them and Officer Porter Walton leaned out of the driver's side window.

"What brings you two out this way?" Porter asked with a smile as he stopped the police car.

Not sure if Jay had told Porter they were meeting Betsy Billings for an interview, Shelly only said, "Breakfast. This place serves a delicious breakfast."

"Too bad you didn't invite me." Porter grinned.

"Next time," Juliet told him.

"Really? I'll hold you to it."

"Anything new with the case?" Shelly asked as tiny glistening snowflakes gathered over the shoulders of her winter jacket.

"I'm sure Jay is keeping you abreast of things." Porter gave a shrug. "That's double-speak for nothing is new."

"We were biking on the mountain trails yesterday," Juliet said. "We saw you down by the barn."

Porter's eyes widened. "When? Yesterday? Yeah. I went out to have another look around. Where were you?"

"Up on the ridge trail," Shelly said. "Did you find anything? See anything that might help the case?" She didn't understand why, but a feeling of alarm grabbed at her stomach.

Porter shook his head. "I was just trying to get a feel for the place."

"Did you see anything in the snow?" Juliet asked. "Any traces of footprints?"

"Nothing," Porter said. "I'd better get going. See you later."

The police car drove away and Shelly walked up to a parked car and tugged on the handle to open the door. "Why won't it unlock?"

Juliet was walking further along and she looked at her friend and giggled. "Because it's not my car. Mine is one aisle down."

"Oh. I thought it was your car." Shelly stared at the small sedan she'd been trying to get into. "It looks just like yours."

Juliet shook her head with a smile. "Somewhat. Mine's in worse shape."

Taking a few steps away from the car, Shelly stopped and glanced back at it ... something tugging at her.

"You can stare at it all you want," Juliet chuckled. "But it still isn't my car."

"Right." Shelly shook herself trying to throw off the odd sensation she was experiencing, and whispered, "I guess."

9

The sun had dropped behind the pine trees when Juliet and Shelly were leaving their resort jobs for the day and heading for the parking lot for the short drive home.

"Try not to bust into someone else's car today," Juliet said with a grin.

"Ha ha," Shelly deadpanned. "The two cars looked similar. Anyone could make the mistake."

A tall man walking towards them called their names and raised a hand in greeting.

"Afternoon, Detective," Juliet said to Andrew Walton.

"Afternoon. Are you leaving for the day?" Andrew asked them.

"I just finished up at the bakery," Shelly said. "I started work early this morning."

Juliet pulled the zipper of her jacket up to her chin. "My last adventure tour got canceled. We're both on our way home."

"Care to take a detour?" Andrew asked. "I'm going over to the barn. I thought I'd walk around, take a stroll into the woods, try to get a feel for the surroundings."

Juliet and Shelly exchanged a quick look.

"I guess we could." Shelly removed gloves from her pockets and slipped them on.

"Your cousin was doing the same thing the other day," Juliet pointed out.

"Porter? He was at the barn recently?" Andrew asked.

"He was looking around. He was standing in a grove of trees. We weren't close enough to speak with him that day, but we saw him the other morning and he said the same thing you did. He wanted to get a feel for the barn and its surroundings."

"I guess we think alike." The tone of Andrew's voice was meant to convey a light-heartedness that his facial expression didn't match. "Do you want to come along to the barn?"

"Sure," Shelly said. "We have some time before we need to get home."

The path that wound around the resort to the barn was slippery in shaded spots and the three investigators had to watch their step.

"Where did your cousin come from?" Juliet asked.

Andrew glanced at the young woman. "You mean which police department?"

"I mean what's his background."

"Porter was born in Paxton Park," Andrew said. "The family moved to Boston for a couple of years, but then they returned to the area and lived one town over, in Williamsville. Porter went to college in Amherst, then decided to apply for the police academy."

Surprised to hear that Porter was a native of Paxton Park, Juliet asked Andrew, "Did you grow up here, too?"

"Not me. I grew up in central Massachusetts. My family and I came here quite a lot though to visit. Porter's parents moved to Florida when he was in college. He joined the police force in a town outside of Amherst, worked there for about six years before accepting the job here."

"Are you two close?" Shelly asked.

"Not really. We'd ski together when my family came out here for a visit. We hadn't seen each other for years. We all lost touch." Andrew shrugged.

"How did you end up in Paxton Park?" Shelly questioned.

Something passed over Andrew's face for a moment. "I worked in Boston for almost ten years. I saw the posting for this position and decided to make a move. I was tired of the city."

"Shelly lived in Boston most of her life," Juliet said.

Andrew took a look at the dark-haired young woman with the slight limp. Shelly knew Andrew was familiar with the car accident that took her twin sister's life and she didn't want him saying a word about it so she spoke quickly, "I prefer the country. The part-time baking job opened up. I didn't want to work full-time anymore so I applied."

"And here you are," Andrew said with a smile.

"Yes, here I am." Shelly hurriedly changed the topic of conversation so Andrew wouldn't bring up the car accident. "What do you hope to see by walking around the barn?"

Andrew let out a breath. "I don't have any expectations. I like to look around the scene of a crime. Sometimes during the initial investigation, things get overlooked. It's important to have a second or third visit. I've had more than one idea pop into my head after returning to a crime scene."

Approaching the barn, Shelly could feel a nervous chill run over her skin and she hoped they would concentrate their efforts outside and not enter the building. When Andrew led the way to the rear of the place, she let out a sigh of relief.

"I'm guessing the robber or robbers parked a vehicle in the woods somewhere," Andrew said. "They couldn't very well drag the safe down to the parking lot so they must have stashed a get-away car back here someplace."

"Nobody noticed any tire tracks though," Juliet said.

Andrew walked the periphery of the building, his gaze pinned on the ground. "It snowed after the robbers would have taken off. Prints could have been obscured by the snowfall."

"I don't know," Juliet said. "It didn't snow heavily enough that prints would be fully obscured."

"Has anyone come forward saying they noticed a car parked back behind the barn?" Shelly asked.

"Not yet," Andrew said as he started for the trails in the woods with the snow crunching under his feet. "The fire roads run off this way through the forest."

Juliet nodded. "If the robbers parked on a fire road, they still would have had to drag the safe out of the building and along the trails before they got back to their car."

"That would be a lot of work." Shelly's leg began to ache from trudging along the snowy trail. "Unless...."

Andrew stopped walking and turned around. "Unless what?"

"Unless they brought along a toboggan."

"A toboggan?" Andrew looked confused for a second.

"You're a genius." Juliet beamed at her friend. "A toboggan wouldn't sink much into the snow. They could have put the safe on a toboggan and pulled it into the woods. It would move fairly easily over the snow."

"What if the robbers wore cross country skis?" Shelly asked. "That would eliminate footprints. The skis would leave a mark behind, but the snowfall would have easily covered that up. I bet the snowfall would have hidden the toboggan tracks, too."

Andrew stared at Shelly. "Clever. Very clever."

"But," Shelly said, her eyes narrowed, "the

robbers couldn't have counted on it snowing while the crime was being committed."

"Maybe they didn't care if their footprints were visible?" Juliet thought out loud.

Andrew trained his eyes on the trail and trees, and then glanced back towards the barn. "There are probably always marks in the snow around here what with the heavy machinery moving around all the time. The snow machines, the ski slope grooming equipment, trucks, workers' footprints. The robbers must have known all that. They didn't need to hide their footprints or the tire marks of their vehicle."

"So that means the robbers would have cased the place," Juliet said. "They would have been here to check out where to park, to see if the area was usually covered in tire tracks and footprints."

"Or," Shelly said softly, "someone here told the robbers that the snow was always disturbed around the building."

Andrew added another suggestion. "Or someone who *worked* here was actually in on the robbery."

A FIRE CRACKLED in the fireplace, soft music played,

and Shelly and Justice curled up on the sofa with a cozy blanket. Shelly's eyes kept snapping shut as she petted the Calico cat's fur.

After returning home from walking around the barn with Juliet and Andrew, Shelly was chilled to the bone so she took a long, hot shower, heated up some leftover stew, fed the cat, and then the two retired to their spots in front of the dancing fire to rest.

Thinking over her, Juliet's, and Andrew's walk around the barn and surrounding wooded trails, Shelly cringed each time she considered that an employee of the barn might have had something to do with the robbery and murders.

Hoping the killer wasn't a resort employee or that one of the workers fed information to the perpetrator, Shelly considered other possibilities.

The robbers could have been deliverymen or suppliers who visited the building on occasion.

The criminal might have been a visitor to the resort who overheard something about the money in the safe and plotted a way to steal it.

Shelly watched some sparks from the fireplace log flash and die out and she let out a sigh as her heavy lids dropped down over her eyes. She fell into sleep and began to dream.

Walking through a cold, icy parking lot, Shelly tried to open the door of a car without success. She glanced around and her heart sank. Every car in the lot was the same make, model, and color. She tried the door of the next car, and the next, until she was running through the lot, panicked and anxious, trying to find the right vehicle.

Suddenly she stopped.

Her sister, smiling at her, stood a few cars away, bundled in a winter coat and hat.

Lauren.

Lauren lifted her hand, gestured to Shelly, and then pointed to a car. Shelly slowly walked to the vehicle her sister had indicated, took hold of the door handle, and tugged. It opened for her.

Lauren smiled and turned around.

"Don't go," Shelly called.

Her sister glanced back over her shoulder, gave Shelly a loving look, then took several steps away and disappeared.

Shelly woke with a start and sat up straight nearly knocking the cat from her lap.

Justice gave her owner a withering stare, stepped in a circle on Shelly's lap, and settled down again.

"Sorry," Shelly said to the Calico. "I had a dream. Lauren was in it." She took some deep breaths trying to calm her racing heart. "Everything looked the same. All the cars were similar. I couldn't find the right one. I started to panic. Lauren helped me."

Justice trilled softly and gave Shelly a lick on the hand.

Shelly rested her head against the sofa back and whispered, "Lauren helped me."

10

Shannon Flay, a twenty-eight-year-old curvy blonde with big brown eyes, sat at the beat-up wooden table in the small, cramped conference room of the police station with Shelly and Juliet sitting across from her.

"Your sister already interviewed me," Shannon announced pushing a strand of her shoulder-length blond hair from her forehead. "I didn't know I had to speak with the police more than once."

Shelly gave the woman a friendly smile. "It's helpful for investigators to meet with people more than once. Sometimes things are remembered that were previously overlooked or another detail comes up."

"I don't know anything about the murders," Shannon stated flatly.

Juliet ignored the protests and asked a question. "How long have you worked for the resort?"

"Ten years. Not always as a bookkeeper. I had a couple of other jobs."

And how long have you been working as the bookkeeper at the barn?"

"Five years."

"Is it a good place to work?" Juliet asked.

"It's fine." Shannon leaned back from the table in a move that was probably intended to get her as far away from the interviewers as possible.

"You get along with the other workers?" Shelly asked.

"Sure."

Shelly thought the short answers and slightly resentful attitude might result in them discovering nothing, but she pressed on. "Were you friendly with Grant and Benny?"

"Sure, I was. I saw them every day at work."

"It must be very upsetting for you," Shelly said to the woman.

"Of course it is." Shannon didn't appear very broken up about the murder of her coworkers.

"Had you noticed any tension between people at work?" Juliet questioned.

"Tension?" Shannon cocked her head to the side.

"Disagreements? Arguments? Annoyances?"

Shannon scrunched up her nose. "That's always going on in a workplace full of men."

"Any more than usual happening between people?" Shelly asked.

"I don't think so."

Shelly asked a follow-up question. "What sorts of disagreements usually go on?"

"Oh, little things. Part of someone's lunch gets eaten. Someone didn't fill the gas tank of one of the trucks. A guy didn't clean off the snow machine. It's petty squabbles, nothing major. It's the same in every work environment."

"Did some of the guys squabble more than others?"

"Grant did," Shannon sniffed. "He had been there a long time and thought he was in charge of things. He wasn't. Paul Prince squabbled, too. He was never very happy. He had a sour disposition."

"Did Grant and Paul get into arguments?" Shelly asked.

"Sometimes. Nothing major. They avoided each other for the most part."

"What about Benny?" Juliet questioned.

"Benny was easy-going. He was easy to get along with. Nothing was a big deal with Benny. If something was wrong, he fixed it. He didn't point the finger at anybody."

"Was it hard working with all men?" Juliet asked.

Shannon's eyebrow went up. "I'm not the only woman. Rosa works in the office, too. She's the receptionist and clerk."

"Has she worked there long?"

"About a year? She was hired a few years after me," Shannon said.

"Do the two of you get along?"

"Rosa is quiet. We aren't best buddies or anything but, yeah, we get along fine."

"Did anything out of the ordinary happen before Grant and Benny got killed?" Shelly asked.

Shannon's brown eyes clouded over in confusion. "Like what? What do you mean?"

Juliet leaned forward a little. "Did anyone new show up to the office? Did anyone seem to linger around the place? Was there anyone who was asking questions about how things ran in the office?"

"I don't think so. I don't remember anything like that."

"You should have been in the office on the morning of the murders. Is that right?" Shelly asked.

Shannon sat up straight with a defensive look on her face. "I was sick."

"Did you wake up feeling sick?" Juliet asked.

"I left work early on Friday. I had a fever. I took some medicine and went to bed early. I didn't feel right all weekend. On Monday morning, I didn't feel any better so I took a sick day."

"It was lucky you weren't in the office," Juliet told her.

"What's that supposed to mean?" Shannon asked with angry tone. "You think I didn't go into work that day on purpose?"

"Not at all." Juliet used a soothing voice. "I only meant it was fortunate that you weren't there when the robbers arrived."

A pout formed on the young woman's face. "Troy wasn't there either. He was supposed to be there then, too." Shannon made eye contact with Juliet and Shelly and then said pointedly, "He *overslept*."

"You don't think he overslept?" Shelly asked.

Shannon crossed her arms over her chest. "He never has before. Not since I've been working at the barn."

"Do you think he stayed home deliberately?"

"I have no idea. I only know he wasn't at work when he was supposed to be. Conveniently."

Juliet asked, "Who had access to the safe?"

"Me and Troy. The head business manager did, too, but he was never around."

"Has anyone ever asked you about the safe? How much money was inside on a regular basis?"

"No." Shannon answered before Shelly could finish asking the question.

"No one brought things like that up around you? Maybe when you were out at a bar or a party or something?" Shelly asked.

"No. I don't like to talk about work on my free time so if someone did ask me a question like that, I'd ignore him."

"Did you ever hear one of the barn workers talking about the safe or the money?" Shelly asked. "Even if they seemed to be kidding around about it?"

"I don't remember hearing anything like that."

"You were friendly with Grant?" Juliet brought up the question that was on her and Shelly's minds.

Shannon's lips pursed together and she stared at Juliet. She had to have known the topic would come up, but her expression seemed to indicate that she was surprised by the bluntness of how it was asked. "Yes."

"Were you more than friends?" Shelly asked.

Shannon blew a breath of air out of her nose. "You must know I was."

"How long did you see Grant?"

"Oh, I don't know exactly. Maybe six months?"

"Were you still seeing him at the time of his death?"

"We'd broken off with one another before the robbery." The young woman did not show any remorse over her affair with a married man.

"When did the affair end?"

"It wasn't an affair," Shannon said. "We had a little thing. No big deal. I had no designs on Grant. I didn't want a permanent relationship with him. We had a little fun together. That was it."

"Who decided the fun should end?" Juliet used the woman's own words to phrase the question.

"It was mutual," Shannon said.

"One of you must have broached the subject first," Juliet said.

"Maybe it was Grant." Shannon pushed at her hair. "I really don't recall."

"Why did Grant want to end it?"

"How do I know?" Shannon asked with some force to her voice.

"He might have told you why," Shelly said softly.

"He didn't. He just said it was time to end things. So what?"

"Were you upset about it?"

Shannon leaned forward with daggers coming out of her eyes and emphasized each syllable of her answer. "I ... didn't ... care."

"Had you ever had an affair before?" Juliet asked.

"That's none of your business." Shannon sat back against the chair.

"Did you have an affair with anyone else who worked at the barn?"

"Why is that relevant?"

"Because it could have implications," Shelly said.

"What kind of *implications*?" Shannon sounded testy.

"That's up to the police to decide," Shelly told the woman. "We only do the interviews and report the information to the officers."

"Did you have an affair with any other workers?" Juliet asked the question that Shannon had not answered.

"I slept with a couple of them. It was short-lived."

"Would you tell us who they are?"

Shannon huffed and reported two names, and then she added, "I'm seeing the new guy, Finny, at the moment. He isn't married or anything."

"How did Grant get along with Finny?" Shelly asked.

"He didn't like him. Who knows why?" Shannon glanced up at the clock. "I need to get to work. Is there anything else?"

Shelly thanked the woman for coming in and the interview ended with Shannon leaving the conference room and shutting the door hard behind her.

"Well," Juliet said. "Who knew so much was going on at the barn?"

Shelly rolled her eyes. "There are a lot of things to talk over with Jay. I'm glad we're getting together for dinner tonight."

Juliet picked up on her friend's nonverbal communication. "Is everything okay?"

With a sigh, Shelly said, "I had a dream last night."

"Oh." Juliet sat up in her chair.

"I fell asleep on the sofa with Justice. I dreamt of Lauren."

"What happened in it?" Juliet asked with a quiet voice.

Shelly gave an account of the dream. "I know it came from trying to get into the car that looked like yours in the parking lot the other day." Making eye contact with Juliet, she asked, "But why did it come into my head when I was sleeping? And why did Lauren show up in the dream?"

"You think it has something to do with this case?" Juliet asked.

Shelly looked down at her hands. "Lauren only shows up when I need help."

"What could the importance be?" Juliet thought out loud. "It was a simple mistake. You thought the car was mine because they looked alike. What is the dream trying to tell you? What is Lauren trying to tell you?"

Shelly shook her head and shrugged.

"How did you feel in the dream?"

"I felt anxious. Worried. There were hundreds of cars and they all looked the same. How was I going to figure out which one was yours? I started to panic, and then Lauren showed up and pointed to the right one."

"And then she disappeared?" Juliet asked.

"I asked her to stay. She looked back at me with a smile. It made me feel like everything would be okay."

"Do you have any ideas what it could mean?"

Shelly took in a long breath. "I have no idea."

11

Jay stirred some cream into her coffee. "We're looking at two guys who made deliveries to the barn over the past month. They were new drivers. So far nothing comes up on one of them, but we haven't determined the second man's whereabouts for the time of the crime."

After Juliet removed a chicken pot pie from the oven and set it on the counter to rest, she returned to the table to finish her bowl of cream of cauliflower soup. "What about people who work at the barn? Are any of those people considered suspects?"

"We have people on our radar." Jay set down her soup spoon and complimented her sister's cooking. Looking from Juliet to Shelly, she said, "Tell me your thoughts from the interviews you've done. I've read the reports you put together, but I'd like to hear what you think."

Justice came into the small dining room and rubbed her face against her owner's legs. Reaching down to pet the cat's head, Shelly spoke first. "Shannon Flay didn't seem too upset that her co-workers had been murdered. Maybe that's just how she is, or maybe she had some hand in the crime. She could have given the robbers information about the safe, the time people arrived at work, things like that."

Juliet said, "Shannon might not have pulled the trigger, but she might have been involved in some way. She could be guilty by association."

"Shannon bristled a bit when the topic of being friendly with some of the men came up." Shelly cleared the empty soup bowls while Juliet brought the chicken pie to the table. "She claims Grant initiated the end of their relationship. She told us she didn't care that they broke up."

"Shannon is seeing the new guy, Finny," Juliet reported.

One of Jay's eyebrows raised. "I didn't know that. Shannon moves fast. We should all have a conversation with the new worker."

"I'm also suspicious of Shannon for calling out sick on the morning of the murders," Juliet said. "It's possible she really was ill, but the timing? Pretty convenient."

"Shannon told us Grant got into tiffs with some of the other workers," Shelly said. "She said Grant liked to complain. She told us Grant didn't like Finny. That might have been because Finny was now dating Shannon."

"She also made a comment about Troy Broad-moor oversleeping that morning. It seems she doesn't believe him." Juliet served the pot pie to her sister and her friend and then glanced down at the Calico. "It's too hot, Justice. I'll give you some of the chicken when it cools down."

The pretty cat trilled at the woman.

"What do you think about Troy?" Shelly asked Jay. "Do you think he's telling the truth? He was on the edge when we saw him right after the murders. He was really shaken up."

Narrowing her eyes, Juliet asked, "Do you think he was upset because two co-workers got killed or because *he* murdered them and was fearful of getting caught?"

"We need more information before I can answer that question." Jay lifted her fork to her mouth.

"He's a possible suspect?" Shelly asked.

"Heck," Jay sighed. "Almost everyone is a possible suspect."

"Shannon mentioned a co-worker, Rosa. I didn't know two women worked at the barn. I thought Shannon was the only woman there."

"Rosa Perkins works as a receptionist," Jay said. "She has other clerical duties, as well. She's in her mid-twenties. I spoke with her. She was quiet, seemed frightened by the proceedings, horrified that the two guys had been killed."

"Did she share anything of importance?" Shelly asked.

"No, she didn't." Jay sipped from her water glass. "Rosa might be someone you should have a chat with. She might be more relaxed with you as opposed to talking to a police officer. She might remember something."

"Andrew told us his cousin was born in Paxton Park," Juliet said.

"I remember that from his application," Jay said. "He lived in Boston for a few years and then the family moved to Williamsville."

"I wonder if he knew Grant or Benny," Shelly asked. "They're all around the same age."

"He never mentioned knowing them," Juliet said. "If he'd known the guys, wouldn't he have said so?"

"I'll ask him about it," Jay said reaching for her coffee cup.

Juliet gave her friend a little kick under the table urging her to tell Jay about the dream.

Shelly bit her lower lip, and took a deep breath. "I had a dream the other night."

Jay's cup almost slipped from her grasp. Keeping her voice even, she asked, "Did you?"

Shelly gave a nod. "It's probably a bunch of nothing, but I thought I should say something to you."

"Good," Jay nodded. "I'm glad you brought it up. Can you tell me about it?"

Shelly gave a quick account of her dream of being in a parking lot with a hundred cars that all looked alike. "I couldn't find the one I wanted ... until, Lauren showed up and helped me."

"You felt panicky before seeing your sister in the dream?"

"Yes." Shelly's voice was soft.

"And after you saw her? Did your anxious feelings pass?" Jay asked.

"I felt like things would be okay. I knew she'd help me if I needed her." Shelly sighed. "I wanted her to stay, but she just smiled at me and disappeared."

"Do you have a sense of what the dream might mean?" Jay asked. "What your sister was trying to tell you?"

"No." Shelly's long brown hair moved gently over her shoulders as she shook her head. "I suppose it might not mean anything. It might have been only a dream with my sister in it."

"Has Lauren been in some of your regular dreams?" Jay asked.

"Not so far," Shelly admitted. "I guess my brain could be telling me that some things aren't what I think they are? Like I thought I was trying to get into Juliet's car, but it belonged to someone else and only looked like hers."

"Okay," Jay said kindly. "That makes a lot of sense. It's an interesting development. I wouldn't spend too much time trying to figure it out. It seems best not push this kind of thing. Let it play out as it will. At night, your mind is working on what you see and hear during the day. It's trying to interpret the information. It will all become clearer over time."

Talking with Jay about her dreams almost always made Shelly feel better about them. Jay treated Shelly's dream experience as completely within the range of normal abilities even though part of her thought there might be something extraordinary about them.

"What are the next steps?" Juliet asked her sister. "How can we help? What should we do next?"

"I think we should speak with Troy Broadmoor again," Jay said. "I'd like to pull more details from him about the everyday operations at the barn. Ask about the people who come and go. Find out the daily routine. It would help if the two of you came along."

The women decided when it would be best to pay the man a visit. He still hadn't returned to work due to his anxiety over being in the room where the murders took place. Management was creating a plan to move Troy into a new office a few doors down the hall from his previous one in the hope that a new space would help ease him back into his job.

"I sure wouldn't be able to return to my job if it meant I had to work in a room where two of my co-workers had been shot to death," Juliet said with a shake of her head.

"Management is reconfiguring the office spaces so no one has to work in that particular space," Jay said. "It's the best they can do. They certainly won't consider knocking down the whole building and constructing something new."

Justice let out a low growl.

"I hadn't thought about that," Shelly admitted. "It would be horrible to go back to work in that place."

"How do you feel about going in there?" Jay eyed Shelly wondering if the young woman would be able to return to the space where she came upon two murdered men.

A shiver ran down Shelly's back. "Do you want me to go inside?"

"Would you mind?" Jay asked. "I'd like to speak with the new employee, Finny, as well as the receptionist, Rosa. I'd like to talk to them at the barn, in their work environment."

"Okay. Sure. I'll go with you." Shelly ran a hand up and down her arms to banish the goosebumps that had formed and a thought popped into her head. "Remember when we went with you to see Troy Broadmoor? He seemed on the verge of a nervous breakdown. He kept saying, *I didn't see anything*. Why would he keep repeating that?"

"He was in shock," Jay reminded Shelly. "He may not even have known what he was saying."

"Why did that come into your mind?" Juliet watched her friend's expression.

Justice jumped onto one of the chairs and kept her eyes glued on Shelly.

"I don't know why," Shelly said. "But if Troy *didn't* see anything, why did he have to keep saying so. Was he trying to convince himself that he hadn't seen anything?"

Juliet leaned forward, her eyes dark and questioning. "Or was Troy trying to convince everyone else?"

12

———

Jack and Shelly spent the windy, cold afternoon skiing together on the slopes. Jack praised his girlfriend for having the tenacity to attempt something she'd been afraid to do worrying her leg would prevent her from being able to manage the mountain.

After the last run, Shelly beamed at Jack, her cheeks rosy and her eyes bright. "I'm happy. It was so much fun. I loved it."

When Jack wrapped her in his arms, their skis overlapped and almost caused them to slip and fall. The two laughed out loud at their near tumble onto the snow.

"We've skied for two hours without incident,

then we get to the bottom and get tangled up together," Jack said.

"Well, there are worse things than getting tangled up with you." Shelly smiled and Jack carefully leaned forward to plant a kiss on her lips.

Sitting near the fire in the lodge, they sipped hot chocolate and ate pieces of apple crisp with vanilla ice cream. Shelly was still talking about how great it had been flying down the mountain trails. "It was awesome."

"It makes me happy to see you so happy." Jack lifted his steaming mug and blew on the contents to cool it. "We should try the snow tube park one of these days."

"I'd love that." Shelly licked a little ice cream from her fork. "Thanks for asking me to ski today. It's made me feel much better. The case was dragging me down."

"I hate to bring it up, but how are things going?" Jack removed his thick ski sweater and placed it on his chair.

"Slow." Shelly shook her head. "We've interviewed a few people. There's nothing definitive yet."

"Do you have the sense the attempted robbery was random?" Jack asked.

"I don't know." Shelly's face looked pensive. "I

have no reason or evidence to lean one way or the other yet." She glanced around to see if anyone nearby was listening. "But I *am* leaning in a certain direction. I have the feeling that the murders weren't random and I think someone or some people at the barn were in on the robbery or knew it was going to happen."

"Really? What makes you think so?"

Taking a deep breath, Shelly said, "My intuition makes me think so. It might turn out to be wrong, but right now, I think someone at the barn knows some details, but isn't telling."

"Will you interview more people?" Jack asked.

"Yes. Some of the workers from the barn." Shelly ate the last bite of the apple crisp. "That was delicious. I was starving."

"The ice cold temperatures and the exercise always make me hungry," Jack admitted. "I hope you or Jay can find some clues. Something that turns the case."

"When you talk to people who are touched by a crime like this, it's often hard to sort the truth from the fiction we get told." Shelly pushed her hair from her eyes. "It would be really helpful if people would stop trying to hide little things they think will tarnish the deceased's memory. Nobody's perfect.

Keeping details from us only serves to conceal clues and makes it harder to solve the puzzle."

"It's human nature, I guess."

"What do you know about Grant and Benny?" Shelly asked. "You told me you weren't surprised to hear the guys got caught up in this mess."

"You know some people just seem to be risk-takers? They don't seem to think things out, what can go wrong, what the consequences might be for their actions? Grant always seemed impulsive. If something sounded like fun, he'd leap at it. He liked women. He saw other women besides his wife. I know the rumor was that his wife didn't care if Grant spent time with other women, and I heard Emmy had a fling or two of her own, but...." Jack hesitated and then said, "I don't know, but I think being with other people besides your spouse can be damaging to the relationship. Grant was the kind of guy who wouldn't think beyond the moment."

"What about Benny?" Shelly asked.

"I think he was different than Grant. I never heard Benny was seeing other women. He seemed happy, content with his girlfriend and his life. He wasn't the type to need that rush of adrenaline that Grant seemed to crave. Benny seemed like a people-pleaser. It makes me wonder if he got dragged into something he wasn't expecting. Maybe he'd go along with something a friend asked him to because he didn't want to let the friend down."

"It's interesting to get your take on the two men," Shelly said.

Jack checked his watch. "We should get going and deliver that lunchbox to Emmy."

Jay had Grant's lunchbox in her car with the intention of returning it to his wife. The box had been checked over by police and they were ready to release it. When Jay and Shelly met for dinner at Juliet's house, Shelly offered to take the lunchbox to Emmy since Jay had meetings all day long and into the evening. "Jack won't mind driving me over there."

"Are you okay about riding in my truck?" Jack asked with a kind tone. "I can do the errand on my own if being in the vehicle will make you uneasy."

Shelly stood and put her ski parka on. "It's always easier for me when I ride with you. I would like to avoid it, but that's just putting my head in the sand. I have to desensitize myself and get accustomed to riding in cars again. I hate it, but I have to face my fears."

Jack nodded and took her hand and they headed

out to the truck to make the short drive to the house where Grant's wife, Emmy, now lived alone.

After knocking on the door, Emmy invited Jack and Shelly in out of the cold.

Shelly handed a paper bag to the woman. "Officer Landers-Smyth asked me to drop this off to you."

Emmy's facial muscles seemed soft and loose and she looked like she might burst into tears at any moment. "Thanks." She took the bag from Shelly. "I don't know why I told Officer Smyth I wanted the lunchbox returned. It makes me sad. I should have told her to throw it out."

"Would you rather I take it back with me?" Shelly offered.

"No." Emmy said the word with a force that surprised her. "I'll keep it." Her voice had gone soft again.

"How are you, Emmy?" Jack asked. "Is there anything I can do for you? I'd be glad to plow your driveway whenever it snows."

Emmy batted away a tear that threatened to fall. "Thanks, but the husband of a friend is doing it for me."

"Don't hesitate if there's anything you need," Jack

said. "Just call the resort and they'll connect me or leave me a message."

"Thanks." Emmy shifted on her feet. "Oh, can I get you something to drink? Some cookies or something? I'm forgetful lately. I feel like I'm moving around in a fog."

"No, thanks. We had something to eat a little while ago." Shelly smiled kindly. "It's understandable to be fuzzy-headed. It's normal ... under the circumstances."

"Yeah, I guess." Emmy opened the paper bag and took out the lunchbox, setting it on the kitchen counter. She stared at it for several moments and Shelly thought the woman might break down, but instead, Emmy turned to her and blinked. "This isn't Grant's lunchbox."

Shelly looked from the lunchbox to Emmy. "It was in the refrigerator at the barn. Grant left it in there on the morning of the crime."

"Maybe he left it in the fridge, but this isn't it."

"Didn't he own a black metal lunch container?" Shelly asked feeling confused about what Emmy was telling her.

Emmy gave a slight nod. "Yes. I always wanted to get rid of it, buy him a new one, but no, Grant had to keep the one he had." The woman gestured to the box. "This isn't it."

"Why do you say that? It's black. Metal. It was in the refrigerator at the barn. I saw it in there right after the crime took place."

Emmy cocked her head. "The police must have mixed it up with this one. This isn't Grant's. His was a little more beat-up. His had a slash across the side. The metal got scraped. There isn't a scrape on this one."

"Well, I don't know." Shelly's mind raced. "I suppose the police might have sent the wrong one."

Emmy opened the box. "Nope. This definitely isn't Grant's. His was stainless steel inside. This one is black."

Shelly peered over the woman's shoulder to see. "I'll have to ask Officer Smyth about it. You're sure this isn't Grant's?" As soon as she asked the question, Shelly realized how foolish it was. The woman knew her husband's lunchbox. When they were here previously, Emmy told them she made Grant's lunch every day. She would have handled the box every morning before Grant left for work.

"I'll bring it back to the police station," Shelly said. "I'm sorry to inconvenience you. Sorry about the mix-up. I'm sure they'll be able to locate your husband's lunchbox."

"Thanks." Emmy passed her hand over her eyes. "I shouldn't even want the old banged-up thing. But I do."

When they left the house and crunched over the snow on the way to the truck, Jack said, "That's odd. Are there two similar lunchboxes at the police station? How could they have mixed them up? Could they have misplaced the box?"

"I hope they didn't lose it," Shelly moaned. "Emmy lost her husband. She doesn't need to lose any of the things that belonged to him, too."

Shelly took a quick look inside the paper bag.

Two things that were similar, but only one of them belonged to the person in question. A cramp of unease clutched at Shelly's stomach.

13

"Jay told me the lunchbox I brought back after trying to drop it off at Emmy Norris's house is the lunchbox that was in the barn's refrigerator," Shelly told Juliet.

"But Emmy said the box isn't Grant's." Juliet rubbed at her chin. "Could she be mistaken?"

"I don't think so. She said Grant's had a slash mark on one side and the inside of his was stainless steel. The one I brought to her was black inside."

"Well, this is weird." Juliet frowned. "Maybe Grant didn't bring his lunchbox to work that day. Maybe he left it in his truck. The one Jay gave you must belong to someone else at the barn."

Shelly shook her head. "Jay went to the barn with it this morning. No one claimed it."

Narrowing her eyes, Juliet said, "It *might* belong to someone there, but that person might be denying it. For some reason."

Shelly took in a long exasperated breath. "It's a lunchbox, for Pete's sake. What could possibly be the big deal?"

Justice let out a hiss from under the kitchen table.

Shelly lifted her teacup to her lips and drank. When she set it down on the table, she looked her friend in the eyes. "It's odd."

"It sure is," Juliet echoed the sentiment.

"I mean the situation is strange."

Juliet leaned her head slightly to the side in question.

"The other day, I tried to get into your car in the parking lot, but the car I thought was yours belonged to someone else," Shelly explained. "The lunchbox we thought belonged to Grant belongs to someone else. Are these things clues to what's going on?"

Juliet stared with a blank look on her face. "It *is* strange, isn't it? What could it mean?"

"Things may not be what they seem?" Shelly suggested.

"Huh," Juliet said. "Who or what isn't what

it seems?"

Shelly turned her hands palm up in a helpless gesture. "I can't answer that question."

"Then we'd better keep our eyes open. Wide," Juliet said.

"I'M SORRY. I don't recall that you were here before. I was in a bad way." Troy Broadmoor looked a lot better than the last time Shelly had seen the man. He had color in his face and he didn't act like a scared rabbit, but he still appeared to have lost weight which showed in his sunken cheeks and in the dark circles under his tired-looking eyes.

Jay had picked up Shelly and Juliet for the meeting with the barn's office manager at his home.

"It's perfectly okay." Shelly smiled kindly. "How are you doing?"

Troy let out a long sigh and gave a weak smile. "Well, the anti-anxiety medication I'm on has helped. I'm waiting to go back to work. The offices are being remodeled. Nothing fancy, just configuring them in a different way. I'll return on a part-time basis to start with. I'm hoping that being back to a routine will be helpful. It will keep my mind busy." Troy ran a hand over his sandy-blond hair.

"Would you mind running through what happened on the morning of the crime?" Jay asked in a soft voice.

Troy's lips parted and he glanced around the room with a panicked look in his eyes. The women didn't think he was going to be able to answer, but in a few moments, he cleared his throat and said, "I can do that." The statement seemed to be more to convince himself that he was able to recount the events of that morning.

"Thank you, Troy," Jay said. "I know it's difficult. Take your time. Stop when you need to."

Troy nodded. "Roberta had to be at work earlier than usual that morning. I heard her alarm go off and she got up to get ready. I fell back to sleep. I was certain I'd set the other alarm for my waking time, but somehow it didn't go off. Maybe I forgot to set it. Maybe Roberta accidentally turned it off when her alarm went off. We don't know what happened. Whatever the cause, the result was I overslept."

"Roberta left the house before you had to be up?" Shelly asked.

"That's right. When I woke and saw the time, I jumped out of bed and took a quick shower. I grabbed some granola bars and headed out to my car. Snow and ice covered the windshield so I had to clear it before driving away. Finally, I arrived at the barn." All the wind seemed to disappear from the man's sails.

"Did things seem off when you arrived?" Jay asked.

"Off?" Troy shifted his gaze to his hands resting in his lap. "You mean like something was wrong?"

"Did something seem wrong?" Jay asked.

"I didn't think so. Not at first."

"What happened after you arrived at the barn?" Shelly asked.

"I parked, got out of the car, walked to the front door." Troy hesitated. "It was snowing. I...."

The three women sat quietly waiting for Troy to go on and in less than a minute of awkward silence, he did. "I went up the walkway to the front. The door was unlocked. I went in. Our bookkeeper, Shannon Flay, is usually there before me, but not that day. She took a sick day. I didn't know it at the time, but she'd sent me an email telling me she'd be out. Rosa Perkins is our receptionist. She hadn't yet arrived."

"Was Rosa due to be in the office?" Jay asked.

"Not that day. That day of the week she comes in an hour and a half later," Troy said.

"Was anyone else supposed to be there who wasn't?" Shelly asked.

Troy's shoulders slumped. "Grant and Benny."

"Are they usually at work before you get there?" Jay asked.

"Always, yes," Troy said. "At first, I just thought they were out grooming the slopes or making snow. They get to work early. Sometimes they make a quick coffee, and then head to their work. They're always outside when I get to the barn."

"What happened after you went inside?" Jay asked.

Troy's face lost a bit of its color as a sense of panic washed over him. "I went to the kitchen. I put my lunch in the refrigerator. Then I got my coffee mug from the cabinet and was about to pour myself a cup. There was nearly a full pot on the coffee maker. Benny always made coffee as soon as he got to work." The man's chest rose and fell rapidly and he looked far away.

"Did you pour yourself the coffee?" Juliet asked trying to gently bring him back to the conversation.

"What?" Troy blinked. "What did you say?"

"The coffee. You were about to pour yourself a cup of coffee," Julie prodded him.

"Yes," Troy said. "I mean no. I didn't pour the

coffee. I heard something. I thought I heard the back door open. At first, I assumed it was Grant or Benny coming back in for something. I listened. I didn't hear any footsteps so I went out into the hall."

"What did you see?" Jay asked.

"I didn't see anything."

"Did you hear anything?" Jay questioned.

"I didn't hear anything. It was deathly quiet." Troy's mouth opened. "I'm sorry. A poor choice of words."

"What did you do?" Shelly asked.

"I walked towards my office. I wondered if the back door got left open and the wind might have pushed it shut with a bang," Troy said. He seemed to brace himself. His voice became whisper-soft. "As I passed my office, I saw them. On the floor."

"Was anyone else inside the room or in the hall?" Jay asked.

Troy looked at Jay with a blank face. "I didn't see anyone else."

"Did you hear a sound like gunshots?" Jay asked.

Troy considered. "No. I thought the door banged shut. That's the sound I think I heard."

"Was the door blowing in the wind? Did it open and close while you were in the hall?" Shelly asked.

Troy turned his gaze on the young woman. "I

don't remember. As soon as I saw Grant and Benny, I think I went into shock. That's what the doctor told me anyway. I was probably in shock."

"What did you do after you saw the bodies?" Juliet asked.

"I don't know for sure." Troy's eyes glistened with tears. "I remember being outside. It was cold." The man looked from Juliet to Shelly. "You found me outside, didn't you?"

"We heard a scream," Shelly said. "Juliet and I were skiing. We'd just finished a run. We were on the slope close to the barn. We saw you come outside."

Troy nodded, staring off across the room. "Benny and Grant. Who would shoot them? Why not just steal the stupid safe and get out? Why did he have to kill them?"

"Did you notice anything? Did you see anyone inside the building?" Jay asked. "A quick look? A shadow? Anything?"

"I didn't see anything," Troy said in a robotic way.

Shelly recalled Troy had repeated that very same sentence over and over the last time they had come to see him. Troy seemed like a person who had been traumatized by an event and had trouble recalling some of the details of what had happened.

Was Troy impaired by the stress of the situation? Was his brain trying to protect him from his experience? Was someone else in the building? Did Troy maybe get a look at someone?

Shelly sighed.

Was Troy protecting himself by playing the victim of a traumatic event? Could he be protecting someone else? Could Troy have been in on the crime? Did he give someone information about how to get at the safe? Was no one supposed to get hurt? Was the man horrified by the murders of his colleagues because he had something to do with it?

Was Troy a victim of a traumatic event? Or was he only resembling one? Like the two similar cars and the two similar lunchboxes.

Thoughts formed in Shelly's mind.

Don't be fooled by the thing that only *seems* correct. Don't take things at face-value.

14

After her workday at the diner was over, Shelly biked back into town being careful not to hit any icy patches on the road. Some slush on the side of the street got kicked up now and then by her tires, but riding her bike was always preferable to traveling in a car.

Before sitting down at the police station's conference room table, Shelly introduced herself to the young woman already seated, Rosa Perkins. Twenty-five-year- old Rosa had long, wavy, almost black hair that tumbled over her shoulders. Her almond-shaped dark eyes showed intelligence and a hint of caution. Jay had finished speaking with Rosa, but she wanted Shelly to talk with the woman in the hopes she might find out things Rosa didn't want to bring up with a police officer.

"You work at the barn?" Shelly asked. "You're the receptionist?"

"I work as the receptionist and a clerk. I do a little bit of everything." Rosa nodded. "I studied business in school. After I graduated, I worked at the resort as an event planner. I want to go back to school to get my master's degree so I thought I should get as much experience as possible. I asked to be transferred when the barn job opened up. I wanted to get some experience working in the mechanical side of running a resort."

"How do you like working there?" Shelly asked.

"I like it. The guys can be a little crude. They can be funny, too. I like learning the more technical stuff, running the operations."

"Do the guys take you serious?"

Rosa said, "Not all of them do. Troy is helpful though. He knows so much about the resort. He gives me things to work on that broaden my knowledge."

"Shannon Flay works at the barn, too," Shelly said. "How do you get along with her?"

"Fine. We get along fine."

Shelly thought she heard an exception in the woman's voice. "You're friendly?"

"Yes."

"Is Shannon friendly with the guys who work there?" Shelly knew her question could be taken in different ways.

"Shannon gets along with everyone," Rosa said.

"We've heard that Shannon has had relationships with some of the men."

Rosa visibly relaxed. "It's true. I stay out of it. I pretend I don't see or hear anything. I think Shannon thinks I'm naïve."

"Shannon was in a relationship with Grant Norris?" Shelly asked.

"She was, yes."

"Was the relationship ongoing? Were they together at the time of the crime?"

"No, I think they'd broken up about a month before the murders. Shannon is seeing the new guy, Finny Finelli. She tries to hide it, but she doesn't do a good enough job."

"Do you know who broke off the relationship? Was it Grant or Shannon?"

"It was Grant. He had his eye on someone else ... the woman who delivers the vehicle parts to the barn. She's really good-looking."

Shelly asked, "Who does she work for?"

"Automotive and Machinery Solutions," Rosa said. "She's at the barn almost every day dropping off parts and supplies. She started doing the deliveries about two months ago. Before that it was an old guy who brought the parts."

"Do you know her name?"

"Robby-Ann. I don't know her last name."

"Did Grant get along with Finny?" Shelly asked.

Rosa pushed a strand of her hair behind her ear. "Grant liked to boss people around. He wanted Troy's job. He wanted to be the one in charge. Most of the workers just ignored Grant when he tried to tell them what to do. Finny wasn't like that. He didn't listen to Grant's orders. He often told Grant he was wrong. He did his work the way he thought it should be done."

"So there could be some tension between them?"

"Grant would sass Finny, call him out sometimes, but Finny ignored him and went about his business."

Shelly asked, "Was Grant into anything that could have gotten him killed?"

Rosa thought about that, then answered. "I don't know. Grant could be volatile. I don't mean in a physical way. Sometimes he was like a buzzing fly.

He seemed to want to get under some people's skin to get a rise out them. He seemed to like drama. Could that get him into trouble? I bet it could under the right circumstances."

"Did he drink?"

"I'm sure he did, but he didn't drink on the job," Rosa said. "At least, I don't think he did."

"Drugs?"

"I never saw that. Doesn't mean he didn't do it on his own time." Rosa's forehead scrunched. "I saw Grant out at a bar one night. His choice of friends didn't seem that great. They seemed a little scummy, tough guys looking to show off. Not my kind of people. The new guy from the barn, Finny, he was in the bar that night, too. Anyway, Grant was drunk, being loud, fooling around, acting like a jerk being a pest to some women who were there. The bartender called the police. When the officer got there, Grant and his friends were told to leave the place."

"When was this?"

"Oh, let's see. A couple of weeks ago?" Rosa told Shelly. "The same officer who kicked them out is working on this case."

"Officer Landers-Smyth?" Shelly asked.

"Is that the woman I was talking with before you came in? No, not her. It was a man."

"Dark hair or light hair?"

"Light. Good-looking. A nice build. Slim."

"Officer Walton," Shelly said.

"I think I heard someone call him Porter?" Rosa said.

"Yes, that's him."

"Grant looked like he wanted to punch the officer when he was told he had to leave the bar." Rosa leaned forward in her seat. "Thankfully, he had the good sense not to do such a stupid thing. He kind of glared at the officer. I saw Grant say a few things to the cop, but I couldn't hear anything. The officer gave him a look and Grant backed down. I heard him telling Shannon about it the next morning at work. They didn't know I could hear them. Grant said the cop gave him a hard time over nothing. He sounded really angry about it."

After a little more discussion about the incident at the bar, Shelly asked, "No one was at the barn the morning of the robbery and the murders. Troy overslept, Shannon took a sick day, you weren't there either."

Rosa sat straight. "Benny and Grant always started work early."

"Why weren't you at the barn that day?" Shelly

asked, making sure her voice did not carry an accusatory tone.

"I don't go in until later on that day of the week. I only go in early on Tuesdays, Wednesdays, and Thursdays."

"Did anyone at the barn seem on edge before the crime took place? Was anyone acting nervous or distracted?"

"Shannon was a little grouchier than usual. Sometimes we can talk a little, but she seemed annoyed or something so I left her alone," Rosa said.

"What about Grant or Benny?"

"They seemed themselves, I think."

"What about Troy?" Shelly asked. "Did he seem like he had something on his mind?"

"Troy always has things on his mind," Rosa said. "He has to juggle a ton of things. If there were issues with the ski slopes, he'd be in big trouble with management. If the equipment doesn't work, then the ski slopes won't be pristine, and then he'd be in trouble. Everything has to work to make the resort function smoothly. As far as management is concerned, the worst thing is a disappointed or angry guest. Troy's job is incredibly stressful."

"Do you think someone from the barn might have been in on the job?"

Rosa took in a long breath. "My first reaction to that would be *of course, not.* But people can surprise you. I don't know the people I work with that well. Sure, I know them, we talk, we get along, we work together to make things go well. But really? Who knows what goes on in some people's heads? Could someone from the barn commit a robbery? Maybe. Could someone from the barn shoot someone to death? Maybe. Do I suspect someone? No, I don't."

"Do you have access to the safe?"

Rosa's eyes popped. "Me? No. Only Troy and Shannon. Well, the accountant in the main office does, too, I guess."

"I hear the money in the safe wasn't deposited like it should have been," Shelly said.

"Shannon does the deposits. She went home sick on Friday before the money was supposed to go to the bank," Rosa said.

"She was still sick on Monday morning," Shelly pointed out. "She wasn't in the office when the robbery took place."

"That's right." Rosa nodded.

"What was wrong with Shannon?"

"She told me on Friday afternoon she had a fever, felt really tired, had a sore throat and a headache. She must have had a touch of the flu. She went home early. I guess she couldn't shake it off over the weekend."

"Why didn't Troy take the money out of the safe and make the deposit at the bank?" Shelly asked.

"I don't know."

"Was Troy around on Friday?"

"Except for Shannon leaving work early, things were normal. At least in the front office, they were."

"Did you see Troy in the afternoon?" Shelly questioned.

"I don't know. I honestly can't remember," Rosa said. "What with everything that happened on Monday, I've forgotten much of what went on the Friday before."

"Do you work on weekends?" Shelly asked.

"No, I don't. There's only one person in the front office on Saturdays and Sundays. An older woman. Ruth Benson. She's handled the weekends for years."

"How about Troy, or Grant and Benny? Did they work weekends?"

"If something big went wrong, Grant or Benny might have been called in. Other times, they had days off during the week when they had to work any weekend days. I know Troy always drops by on the weekends to make sure everything is okay."

There was something about the conversation that made Shelly think she wasn't giving a particular detail enough attention, but try as she might, she couldn't put her finger on what was picking at her.

"Shannon must be quite upset over Grant's death. Since she was close to him for a while," Shelly said.

One of Rosa's eyebrows went up. "Really? I don't think Shannon seems broken up over Grant's murder at all. She's got a hard edge to her. I don't think she's a very caring person."

15

Shelly and Juliet shared a booth in a popular Paxton Park pub. Some friends played darts, some people stood beside an old-fashioned jukebox, and a few others played pool on the far side of the room. The pub, a gathering spot for locals and tourists, had golden wood walls and a two-story soaring ceiling. The second floor of tables and sofas looked down over the main area of the place. A towering stone fireplace contained a crackling, roaring fire and ceiling fans moved lazily overhead.

"It's mobbed in here tonight," Juliet glanced around the large room at the groups of friends and couples eating appetizers and dinners and enjoying drinks from the bar.

"It's nice to be surrounded by a crowd of happy

people," Shelly said. "It can take our minds off the case."

"Too bad Jack couldn't join us tonight." Juliet raised her wine glass to her lips.

"I know. Jack offered to cover for one of the guides. He wasn't thrilled to have to do the overnight camping tour, but the other guide has helped Jack out so he stepped in to cover for him."

Juliet gave her friend a wink. "Jack's a great guy. I think you found a keeper."

With a laugh, Shelly said, "Don't marry me off quite yet."

Glancing over to the bar, Juliet raised an eyebrow. "Andrew and Porter are here."

"Uh, oh. I hope they don't see us." Shelly hunched down in the booth. "I didn't want to talk about the break-in or the murders tonight."

"Too late. Here they come." Juliet returned Andrew's wave. "Andrew's kind of cute."

Shelly stared at her friend. "Really? But the arrogance."

"He hasn't been that way with us when we're together for the case. Maybe he saves that attitude for the criminals."

"Everyone has the same idea tonight." Andrew smiled at the young women. "Porter and I thought it would be good to get out for a beer and relax for a while."

"I've never seen this place so busy." Porter held his beer glass in one hand as he let his gaze wander over the crowd.

"Mind if we join you?" Andrew asked.

Juliet answered with a smile. "Sure. It's just the two of us."

The men slid into the booth and the foursome engaged in light conversation.

"We heard you were born here in town," Juliet said to Porter.

"Who's spreading rumors about me?" Porter chuckled, and then said, "It's true. I've come full-circle, I guess. Born here, moved away for a while, and now back again."

"You didn't move that far away," Shelly said. "So you must like it around here."

"I think the mountains are in my blood." Porter took a long drink from his glass.

"Did you know Grant or Benny when you were growing up?" Juliet asked.

A fleeting look of surprise passed over Porter's face and was gone. "I knew who they were. We went to the same high school. We didn't interact though. They were three grades ahead of me."

"Did you know about them? Ever hear anything about them?" Shelly asked.

"Sure." Porter shrugged. "Grant was a wise-guy. Bossy, thought he was important. He was good at sports, but not so good at academics. You know how it is in lot of places. Socially, the athletes run the show."

"Did you play sports?" Juliet asked.

"Not organized high school sports. I was on the ski patrol, volunteered at the resort when I was in high school. Skiing and snowboarding were my interests."

"So you're pretty familiar with the resort," Shelly said.

Porter drained his glass and signaled the waiter for another beer. "Sure. The place has expanded and they've added more outdoor attractions like the toboggan runs, but it's pretty much the same as it was when I was working here during high school."

"What did you think of Benny?" Juliet asked.

"Benny seemed like a follower. A nice guy, for sure, but seemed like someone who could go off the rails depending on who he hung around with," Porter said.

Shelly asked, "He hung around with Grant?"

"Yeah." Porter sighed. "That didn't turn out well for him, did it?"

Shelly wondered at Porter's insinuation that Grant was the reason Benny was dead. "Do you think Grant caused what happened to them?"

Porter straightened. "I didn't mean that. I can imagine Grant confronting the robber. Benny was probably kind of a bystander. I don't know what went on in that office. It's just my guess that maybe Grant did something stupid and then all heck broke loose."

Shelly turned to Andrew who had been sipping his drink and listening. "Did you know Grant and Benny back then? You visited Paxton Park with your family. Did you ever run into them?"

Andrew shook his head. "I might have, but if I did, I don't remember them at all from my teen years coming to the mountain. Since I've been working in town, I'd see them out and around. We didn't social-ize. I just knew they worked at the resort."

"What about some of the other people who work at the barn?" Shelly asked. "Like Shannon Flay or Troy Broadmoor?"

"I knew who Shannon was," Porter said. "She was in my high school class."

"Were you friends?" Juliet asked.

Porter said, "No. I think we were in some classes together, but no, she and I didn't interact. We had different circles of friends. I don't know Troy."

"What made you want to be law enforcement officers?" Juliet asked the men.

Andrew gave the pretty brunette a little smile. "I like pushing people around."

When Juliet gave the detective a look of shock, Andrew said, "It's a joke. I don't mean it."

The others gave a laugh.

"I wasn't sure if you meant it or not," Shelly eyed Andrew with a grin.

Andrew said, "I wanted to be an officer ever since I was little and there was a fire in our neighborhood. A police officer gave aid to someone who was pulled from the burning house and saved the person's life. I was struck by how important that officer's work was. I wanted to help people, too."

Porter elbowed his cousin. "How noble," he teased.

"Why did you go into law enforcement?" Juliet asked Porter.

"I wanted to be like my older cousin," Porter said.

"Oh, man." Andrew groaned. "I'm not that much older than you."

"Okay," Porter said. "I'm not going to lie. I thought I'd look good in the uniform."

Chuckles went around the table.

Andrew looked at Shelly. "What made you want to be a baker?"

Shelly said, "I've loved baking since I was a little girl. My sister and I worked together to make the family desserts. I wanted my own business. I was saving up to buy a bakery in Boston." Shelly stopped talking abruptly. The reason why she hadn't achieved her goal got stuck in her throat and she couldn't get the words out.

When she looked up, she noticed an empathetic look of sadness in Andrew's eyes. He'd heard the story of her sister's death.

"Why didn't you buy a place?" Porter asked, not knowing what had happened to Lauren. "Why didn't it work out?"

Shelly gave herself a little shake. "I changed my mind," was all she said.

Porter was about to ask her something else when Andrew spoke first, holding Shelly's eyes. "Things change. Wants and needs change. We make adjustments."

Shelly gave a little nod of agreement.

"What about you?" Porter asked Juliet. "What

made you want to work as an adventure guide and instructor?"

Juliet said, "I've always loved the outdoors. I thought about being a teacher, but I wouldn't want to be cooped up inside all day. So I started working here and loved it. I get to be a teacher of sorts, but my days are spent outside instructing in skiing, snowboarding, kayaking, archery. I get the best of both worlds."

The waiter carried another round of drinks to the table and after Juliet took a sip of hers, she asked Porter again, "Tell us the real reason you became an officer. What drew you to it?"

Porter leaned back and smiled. "Honestly? The money."

"That's actually the real reason I decided on law enforcement, too," Andrew kidded. "A secure job where I could make good money. It was all about the money."

When the men were joking about the good salaries that came with being on the police force, something about it picked at Shelly.

"Well then, you'll both be able to retire soon," Juliet teased them.

Shelly directed a question to Porter. "I heard you had an altercation with Grant at a bar one night a few weeks ago. He was being a jerk. He was drunk."

Porter's face took on a serious expression. "I forgot about that. Yeah. Grant had too much to drink. He was hanging out with some sketchy characters. There was a complaint called in and I answered the call."

"Grant was pretty annoyed about getting kicked out of the bar, I heard," Shelly said.

"Yeah, he was. He went quietly though," Porter said. "Who told you about that?"

"Just someone who was in the bar at the time." Shelly gave a shrug and lifted her glass. "Did you have any other interactions like that with Grant?"

"No. I didn't. That was the only time."

"Did Grant challenge you that night?" Shelly asked.

"How do you mean?" Porter asked.

"Did he seem like he might strike out at you? Did he say anything to you?"

"No, he didn't. I really don't remember the episode that clearly," Porter said. "It was the usual drunk in a bar who needed a cop to discipline him."

Shelly studied Porter's face. She thought that was an interesting way for him to describe the incident with Grant.

16

Shelly closed the oven door after slipping a tin of muffins inside to bake and then returned to her work station in the diner kitchen to start on a pie crust.

Henry and Melody buzzed around doing the early morning tasks to prepare for the first rush of the day. Melody carried some cartons of eggs from the walk-in refrigerator to the cooler next to the grills.

"There hasn't been any new information about what happened to those poor men at the barn," the silver-haired woman said. "I never liked Grant, but my gosh, what a terrible thing. Murdered. Who can believe it?"

Henry brought out loaves of bread and English

muffins and set them on the counter near his grill. "Of all the people in town, Grant would be at the top of the list of men who might get themselves into trouble."

Shelly looked over at the couple. "Why do you say that?"

Henry grunted. "One of our sons was a year ahead of Grant and Benny in high school. Grant was always dancing around trouble. He took a car once and went joy-riding around town with his friends. He claimed he knew the car belonged to his buddy and he even had a key to it. He said he was only playing a prank on his friend. The police weren't inclined to agree, but the pal didn't press charges and sided with Grant."

"I think Grant scared the young man and that's why he didn't want the police to get involved," Melody said.

"Scared him?" Shelly asked. "How?"

"I bet Grant threatened him." Melody shook her head. "There was talk about Grant being involved with drugs, using them, selling them."

Henry said, "Nothing ever stuck to the guy though. He was always pushing the boundary of bad behavior and he always got away with it. Thankfully, our kids steered clear of guys like Grant."

"Was Grant violent?" Shelly asked.

"He got into plenty of fights," Melody said. "Our son told us he had a temper and that most kids wanted to stay away from him. He didn't improve with age either. From what I've heard, Grant was a womanizer, a big drinker, probably into other things, too."

"What about Benny?" Shelly asked as she worked the dough.

"Benny was okay," Henry said. "He got mixed up with the wrong crowd. Followed Grant around, did stupid stuff because of him."

"What do you think happened at the barn?" Shelly asked the couple.

"Maybe it was payback," Henry said taking out his grilling tools. "Maybe Grant pushed the wrong person's buttons and the result was getting shot."

Unease skittered over Shelly's skin causing goosebumps to form. "Really? What in the world could Grant have done to make someone want to kill him?"

"He may have pushed the wrong person too far," Melody said. "It's not hard to set some people off."

"With his background in drugs, Grant might have stepped on the wrong person's toes," Henry said as he set up the bottles of ketchup, relish, and mustard on the counter for easy access.

"Do you think the point of the crime was actually to kill Grant?" Shelly asked in disbelief.

"No, I don't," Henry said. "I think the purpose was to steal the safe. It seems some equipment broke down and Grant and Benny returned to the barn. They ran into the robber. It seems a harsh reaction to gun down two guys. Wouldn't the smarter thing have been to lock Grant and Benny in the office and flee?"

"But the robber got a look at their faces," Melody said. "They would have been able to tell the police who it was or at least, give a good description of the robber."

Henry started the grill and began to cook some sausages. "I think it was revenge for something. Just my opinion."

Shelly wiped the flour from her hands onto a dish towel. "Revenge. That's an interesting theory. I wasn't sure if it might just be a random thing. Grant and Benny caught the thief in the act and the person shot them, but maybe it *was* rage and revenge. Do you know Troy Broadmoor?"

"We know who he is," Melody said. "Some people at our church said the man is taking the killings very hard. I can't imagine going into work and discovering two dead bodies." The woman shivered at the thought. "I was in a book club with Troy's wife, Roberta."

"Are you still in the club?" Shelly asked.

"We stop the club every winter for a couple of months and start up again in the spring," Melody told her. "I haven't seen Roberta since Grant and Benny were killed."

"Do you think Troy could have been in on the break-in?"

Melody's eyebrows shot up. "Troy? Gosh."

Henry looked over his shoulder at Shelly. "Troy wouldn't be the first guy who came to mind to be in on the break-in, but I don't know him well, so who knows? Nothing surprises me anymore. I guess we have to think about motivations. What would possess someone to take a risk and try to steal the safe from the barn? Was the guy desperate for money? Was it the thrill of committing the crime and getting away with it? Did someone force him to do it?"

"All good points," Shelly said. "Figuring out the motivation would help figure out who committed the crime."

"But of course, that's easier said than done."

Henry removed some sausages from the grill and placed them in the warming oven, and then added more to the grill to cook. "It's too bad Grant didn't grow out of his wild streak like that new cop did."

Shelly quickly turned her head to Henry. "Who?"

"The new officer in town. He joined the force about six months ago. Porter something or other." Henry looked to Melody. "What's his last name?"

Melody said, "Walton. He went to the regional high school when Grant and our son attended there."

"Porter Walton?" Shelly's voice held a tone of disbelief. "He had a wild side? How so?"

"He was similar to Grant in some ways," Henry said. "He was as smart as a whip in high school. Our son said Porter never had to study and he aced every exam and written assignment."

"Porter was a year younger than our son," Melody said. "Everyone in the school knew how bright Porter was. He would easily have been the valedictorian, but he was skipping so much school in the spring term that he was almost expelled. The administration wouldn't bestow the honor on him."

"Grant was a senior when Porter was a freshman,

right?" Henry asked his wife. "It's too bad Grant didn't change his ways like Porter did."

"What was Porter doing back then?" Shelly asked.

"Drinking, speeding tickets, hanging around with girls and some troublemaker, probably some drugs thrown in. But he got excellent grades and went to college where he was very successful. The guy turned himself around. Now look at him. A police officer. Impressive."

Shelly hadn't realized the wealth of information she could gather from long-time residents of the town. "Do you know anyone else who works at the barn?"

Melody sighed. "Shannon Flay."

"You know Shannon?" Shelly asked.

"I know people who know her," Melody seemed careful about what she said. "She's a beautiful young woman. Sometimes being too beautiful is a curse."

Shelly made eye contact with Melody. "Why do you say that?"

"I think Shannon coasted on her good looks and didn't work to develop her other characteristics," Melody said. "From conversations, I've gathered Shannon didn't bother applying herself at school. She moves from guy to guy. Her mother tells me she doesn't think Shannon is happy, she doesn't think her daughter has any self-esteem. Shannon's never had a long term relationship. She gets angry or annoyed at someone and dumps him. No one can live up to her high standards." Melody shrugged. "It's kind of a sad story."

"I've heard Shannon and Grant had an affair," Shelly said.

"It's true," Melody told her. "It didn't last long. That's another thing. Grant was always after women even though he was married."

Henry clucked disapprovingly from the grill.

Shelly said, "Didn't Grant and his wife have an open relationship?"

Melody made a face. "What does that even mean? If your partner isn't enough for you then why be married to him or her? It's disrespectful to your partner to run around with other people. If you behave that way, why are you married? Why not stay single? If two people aren't a good match, then don't get married."

"I agree with you," Shelly said, "but maybe that kind of behavior works for some couples?"

"I don't believe it." Melody sniffed.

"His wife seems very upset that Grant was

killed," Shelly said. "They must have loved one another."

Melody shook her head. "I doubt Emmy Norris loved Grant. She loved the money he made and brought home. I know it sounds harsh, but I'm friends with people who know her."

Shelly wasn't sure what to say.

Melody sighed again. "I know the girl's mother. Emmy stole from her a few times, stole from her own mother. It caused a falling out between them, a rift that's never been mended."

"I'm sorry to hear that," Shelly said.

Melody went to the front of the diner to help out the waitstaff, but before long, she poked her head into the backroom. "Shelly. There's someone here asking for you."

"Who is it?" Shelly put some pies in the oven.

"A man, around thirty." Melody took a look back at the man. "Dark hair. He seems a little nervous."

"He didn't tell you his name?"

"It was a different-sounding name. I think he said his name is Finny."

Shelly's eyes widened. "Finny?" Removing her apron, she said, "Please tell him I'll be right out."

17

Finny looked to be around thirty-years old, had dark hair and brown eyes, was about five foot, eight inches tall and had a slim, wiry build. He stood next to an empty booth shifting from foot to foot, his eyes looking over the patrons of the diner, but not really seeing them.

Shelly approached the man and introduced herself. "You work at the barn, right?" She gestured for Finny to sit down and she took the bench opposite him. "Would you like a coffee or something to eat?"

"Um," Finny rubbed his hands on his jeans. "Coffee would be good."

Shelly was about to get up when Melody hurried

over with two mugs of coffee and set them on the table with a nod.

Finny added cream and sugar and stirred while Shelly waited to see what he had to say.

Finny took a swallow. "Good coffee. Oh. Sorry. I'm Finny. I forgot to say that. It's my nickname. My last name is Finelli. My first name is Aldo." He made a face. "You see why I don't use that name." Taking another long swallow, he wiped his mouth with the paper napkin.

When he didn't say anymore, Shelly smiled at him and said, "What brings you to the diner?"

"You." The man had kind eyes and a friendly manner, but he seemed very nervous, almost afraid to speak the reason for his unexpected visit.

"Why me? How can I help?" Shelly asked.

"I work at the barn."

Shelly nodded and wrapped her hands around her mug.

"I have a lot of skills. I've done construction, land surveying, drove a truck for a few years, worked as a mechanic. I pick up jobs like that real fast. I have a knack for them. The resort management asked me to interview for the position at the barn. I heard the money was good so I came in to talk to them and I got hired. They told me my varied skills would be an asset to the resort. Those are the words they used. My *varied skills*. An *asset*." Finny smiled. "That sounds pretty good, doesn't it?"

Shelly said, "It sounds very good. A very nice compliment."

"So I've been working there for about six months. I like the work. It's not doing the same thing every day. I like that. Mix things up, then it's not boring."

"I agree. I like variety, too."

"I heard you worked as a baker for the resort. I went next door to the bakery. They told me to come into the diner," Finny said. "I thought that was weird. If you're a baker, wouldn't I find you in the bakery?"

Shelly explained. "The kitchen is located between the diner and the bakery. I make things for both places. There's more room for me to work on the side closest to the diner so that's where I set myself up to bake."

Finny gave a nod. "Makes sense. I was just wondering."

After waiting a few minutes for Finny to say more, Shelly spoke. "Do you need something baked? For an occasion or something?"

"Me?" The man's eyes went wide. "No, nothing

like that." Finny leaned forward and lowered his voice. "You work for the police, too, right?"

A whoosh of anxiety left Shelly uneasy. "On a part-time basis. They call me in when they need help with research or interviewing."

"I saw you at the barn," Finny told her. "I saw you talking to people."

"I was helping gather information," Shelly said. "The police department is often short-handed."

"It's like that at the barn sometimes. Management wants to reshape the offices. You know ... because the guys got shot in there. They don't want anyone working in that office where the bodies were found. Too creepy." Finny gave a little shudder. "They asked me to help out with the demolition. I'm glad to do it. It saves the resort money. That way they don't have to hire outside workers for everything."

Shelly wondered where the conversation was headed and for a couple of seconds, actually considered that maybe Finny dropped in at the diner for no reason other than to chat.

"So anyway," Finny said. "I was working in that office. It's a good thing they're fixing it up. The floor's a mess. That robber hacked away at it to get the safe out. There's blood on the floor, too. But anyway, I have to pull out the heating baseboards to make way for the changes." Finny glanced around the diner and lowered his voice again. "I found something when I yanked out the baseboards." He put his hand in his pocket and when he removed it, he opened his palm to show Shelly a button.

Shelly took a look at the round, gold button with silver ferns circling the edges and then she lifted her eyes. "You found that?"

"It was under the baseboard." Finny moved his hand in a way that indicated Shelly should take it from him.

"It's from one of those expensive winter coats some people wear," Finny said. "You know the ones? They're from Canada. *Winter Wings.* They cost a bundle. More than I make in a week. Probably more than I make in *two* weeks."

"Did Troy wear a coat like that?" Shelly asked.

Finny guffawed. "You kidding me? He couldn't afford a coat like that. None of us can."

Shelly said, "Maybe the button was under the baseboard for a long time. Maybe it belongs to one of the owners of the resort?"

Finny shook his head. "I vacuumed in that office right before the guys got killed in there. I do a good job. I do under the baseboards. The button wasn't there then."

With her head starting to swim, Shelly asked, "What are you thinking?"

"I'm wondering if the killer was wearing one of those expensive coats." Finny took a quick look around the space to see if anyone was listening.

"When did you vacuum the office?"

"Two days before the break-in," Finny said. "The button wasn't there."

Shelly's mind raced. "Why are you telling *me* this?"

"I heard you're trustworthy." Finny's shoulders slumped.

"Who told you that?"

"I can't say. I saw you helping the police, but you're not a police officer," Finny said.

"Why does that matter?" Shelly asked.

"Because I don't trust the police."

"Why not?"

"I have my reasons." Finny sat back against the booth. "I thought this might be important so I decided to tell you."

Shelly extended her arm to return the button to the man.

Finny shook his head. "Keep it. I don't want it. Show it to someone you think will do the right thing.

If you think it's good for nothing, then throw it away."

While Shelly closed her hand around the button, she thought about fingerprints and how now hers and Finny's were on it. As she slipped it into the pocket of her jeans, she recalled seeing something glitter under the baseboard when she was in there right after the murders. Was this the thing she saw?

Finny said in a whisper, "Maybe Grant or Benny fought the robber. Maybe the button got yanked off the robber's coat in the fight."

"It's a possibility," Shelly agreed.

"Do you think it's important?"

"It could be." Shelly could feel the button in her pocket pressing against her hip. "Did you get along with Grant? I've heard there was some tension between you two."

Finny's eyes widened, but instead of downplaying the topic, he hit it straight on. "I didn't like Grant."

"Why not?"

"He was a bully. Full of himself. Thought he could do no wrong, but a lot of what he did, he could have done better. He liked to flirt with any woman who came into the office. He was a jerk."

"Did you dislike him enough to hurt him?" Shelly used an even tone of voice when she asked.

Finny was unfazed by the question. "I sure didn't like him, but I wouldn't do anything to hurt the guy. It wasn't me who killed them. Besides, I liked Benny."

"Was there anyone at the barn who you think could have hurt Grant and Benny?" Shelly asked.

"I'd say no, but how do I know? I haven't worked there that long. I get along with everybody there … you know, except for Grant. I wouldn't think anyone would do such a thing, but who the heck knows?"

"Are you seeing someone at the barn?" Shelly asked.

Finny blew out some air. "Yeah, okay. I'm seeing Shannon Flay."

Shelly said, "Grant was seeing her before they broke up … I think that was right before you started dating her."

"Yeah, it was," Finny said. "Shannon told me she'd been seeing Grant. In my opinion, not a great choice on her part."

"Do you think Grant was bothered that you and Shannon were dating?"

"I'm sure he was," Finny said. "I don't know who broke up with who. I don't think it's polite to ask about those things. If Grant did the breaking up, I know it still bugged him that Shannon was seeing me."

"How do you know that?"

"Grant would walk by and say rude things to me. I won't repeat what he said. He was like that with Shannon, too. He'd go by her desk and say something rude about me to her. He was trying to get a rise out of me. I wouldn't take the bait."

Shelly asked, "Is there someone at the barn you think I should talk to?"

Finny screwed up his face in thought. "Not really. You or the officers must have talked to everybody by now."

"Did law enforcement talk to you?" Shelly asked.

"Yeah, they did. A woman. She was nice. A detective talked to me, too. I don't remember their names. The detective was a jerk. Oh wait, I think the woman called the detective Andrew. You know him?"

"Not well. Why was he a jerk?"

"He had an attitude." Finny shrugged one shoulder. "Funny ... he reminded me of Grant."

18

"I only work the weekends, but sometimes I get called in during the week to cover for someone." Sitting behind the gray metal desk in the reception room of the barn, Ruth Benson was a no-nonsense kind of person. In her late sixties, she wore her gray hair cut very short to her head, a white collared shirt, tan chinos, no jewelry. "I don't know some of the newer workers, but I'm familiar with the ones who have been working here for a long time."

Juliet and Shelly sat to the side of the desk and had been talking with Ruth for a few minutes.

"How do you like working here?" Juliet asked.

"I've been working here for fifteen years so I must like it well enough." Ruth tapped a pencil on the table for emphasis. "Some days are busy as all get-out and others are like today, no action."

"I would think there would be a full crew here on the weekends," Shelly said. "It must be the two busiest days of the week."

"In the winter, all the days of the week are busy. It's not a skeleton crew working on the weekends. It's almost a full capacity crew. They move around to different tasks, go where they're needed when a problem comes up, maybe with a ski lift or with a bare patch on one of the slopes, a slippery main walkway. The workers are experienced."

"What are your duties?" Shelly asked the woman.

"I check the orders, make phone calls, do some of the payroll work, answer phones, direct the workers when there's an issue somewhere at the resort. Jack-of-all trades, master-of-none."

"You knew Grant and Benny?" Juliet asked.

Ruth paused. "Yes, I did."

"Does it bother you to work here after what happened?"

Ruth squared her shoulders. "Absolutely not. The resort continues to function and we do our jobs to support that."

Shelly thought the answer seemed like something a soldier would say.

Ruth added, "I knew those guys for years. I don't mean to say I'm not upset by what happened to them. It's a terrible thing. But we can't allow fear and worry to keep us from doing what we're supposed to do."

Shelly gave a nod and then asked, "How did you get along with the two men?"

"Benny was a sweetheart. A kind person. A good worker." Ruth sighed. "Grant was a good guy, but he could be difficult. Not with me, of course. I cut him off if he was a smart aleck or whatever. He could be crude, a troublemaker with the other workers. Grant liked drama, excitement, getting under people's skin. Most everyone ignored that behavior in him."

"Did some of the workers get angry with Grant?" Shelly asked.

"Some did, but the tension never lasted very long." A call came in and Ruth had to take it. In a few minutes, she was done. "Grant claimed his comments were a joke, he'd always say he was only joking. I think he thought he *was* joking. I don't think he could read people well. He didn't pick up on non-verbal cues. That deficiency could get him into trouble."

"Was Grant liked here at the barn?" Juliet asked.

"Oh, sure. Everybody just took Grant as he was. Sometimes he'd annoy someone, but it would all blow over. No one held a grudge."

Shelly made eye contact with the woman. "Do you have any theories about what happened here that morning? Who might have broken in?"

Ruth folded her hands together and rested them on the desk top. "The way I see it, theories need to be backed up with evidence. I don't have any."

"But you have theories?" Juliet leaned forward in her chair.

"I might." Ruth's blue eyes moved from woman to woman. "I'm not sure I want to voice them."

"Why not?" Juliet asked.

"I don't have anything concrete to say," Ruth said. "My ideas are just that ... ideas. It would be wrong of me to say something that might lead to useless bother. I don't know anything. Walk around town. You'll hear all kinds of gossip and speculation. People wag their tongues even when they don't know what they're talking about. It can be hurtful. It should be avoided."

"But you work here," Shelly said gently. "You knew the guys. You know the other workers, the vendors who come by to drop off supplies. You know what's going on between the people. You probably know what's going on in their lives. It could help the investigation if you shared some things with us."

"I don't think what I might say could be of any help," Ruth said stubbornly.

"When we gather information," Juliet said, "the little pieces by themselves might not add up to anything."

"But," Shelly chimed in, "when they're all added together, a more complete picture unfolds that can lead us to someone we might not have thought to interview. And that person may provide the all-important piece to solving the puzzle."

"It's like when you're all working here at the barn," Juliet said. "One person can't run the resort alone. It takes a team to get the job done. All the small parts working together."

Ruth frowned and looked down at the top of her desk. "I know what you're saying, but I honestly don't know anything that can make a difference."

"Was Grant getting along with everyone here?" Shelly asked trying to start a dialogue with the woman.

Ruth raised her eyes. "For the most part."

"Was there someone he didn't get along with?"

"Grant and Finny sometimes didn't get along," Ruth admitted.

"Why do you think they didn't?" Juliet asked.

"Two strong personalities," Ruth said. "Strong in different ways though. Grant could be in your face. He could be vocal. Finny had strong ideas about how to do his work, but he was quiet. Sometimes the two men clashed. It wasn't a big deal. They weren't sneering at each other all day long. Things would blow over in a little while."

"What about Shannon?" Shelly asked. "I understand both men dated her."

Ruth raised an eyebrow. "Are we venturing into gossip?"

"Certainly not." Shelly shook her head. "We've heard from reliable sources Shannon had dated both men."

"Not at the same time," Ruth clucked and leveled her eyes at Shelly.

"No. Grant had been seeing her and then they broke off with one another. Shannon started seeing Finny right after that."

"Why bring this up?" Ruth questioned.

"Did you notice if either Grant or Shannon was upset over the breakup?" Juliet asked.

"They both seemed out of sorts for a while," Ruth said. "It's an awkward situation. They both work in the same place. Grant's personality would lend itself to him being angry if Shannon started seeing someone else, especially someone in the same workplace."

"You witnessed Grant being angry?" Shelly asked.

Ruth let out a sigh. "I worked a few days in the office when Rosa was out. Grant was being rude to Shannon. She just let it go, ignored him. We knew his nose was out of joint because Shannon had an interest in someone else."

"Do you think someone who works here knew the robbery was going to take place?" Shelly asked.

Ruth straightened and her face showed a shocked expression. "A resort worker?"

"Do you think someone might have given the robber some important information?"

"No one would do that. Why would someone do that? What would be the gain?" Understanding suddenly dawned on Ruth causing her jaw to drop. "Oh. Someone would share the money with the robber." She shook her head with vigor. "No one here would do such a thing."

"Have you ever seen anyone hanging around

Troy's office? Looking around when Troy wasn't in there?" Shelly asked.

"No. I'm out here in front. I don't go in back where the offices are. Only when Troy calls me in or whatever. I wouldn't have seen anyone doing that," Ruth said.

"How is Rosa to work with?" Juliet asked.

"Rosa's a nice girl," Ruth said. "I saw Grant hanging around her desk sometimes, but Rosa had no interest in him. I'm glad, really. Grant was a ladies' man. He didn't want anything serious."

"He *was* married," Juliet pointed out.

Ruth's lips pinched together for a moment. "Yes, I know and I didn't approve. Rosa deserves someone who doesn't play around like that. Like that police officer." The woman tapped her finger against her chin. "Or is he a detective?"

"Who?" Shelly's interest was sparked.

"I think he *is* a detective. He's a good-looking man," Ruth explained.

"Detective Walton?" Juliet asked. "Andrew Walton?"

"Yes, that's right." Ruth's face brightened.

"The detective was out here interviewing the workers here at the barn," Shelly said. "You saw him talking to Rosa?"

"Yes, when the investigation was going on." Ruth waved her hand in the air. "But I saw them together before the robbery took place. I hoped they were dating."

Shelly noticed the disappointment on Juliet's face. She knew her friend thought Andrew was cute and was developing an interest in him. "Where did you see them?"

"Right here. Outside. On the side of the barn. Rosa never works that late in the day so I thought maybe they had been skiing together or something."

"Was it at night?" Shelly asked.

"Yes. I saw them standing next to the building under the side roof lights. I was on the slope finishing my ski run and as I went by, I spotted them."

"What were they doing?" Juliet asked.

"I went by fairly quickly," Ruth said. "They were talking. Rosa looked like she was pointing to the back of the building. Maybe she was pointing out her car to him? I don't know. I remember thinking Rosa didn't look happy. She looked concerned about something."

"When was this?" Juliet asked.

"Oh, a couple of days before the robbery happened," Ruth said.

Shelly felt a tiny wave of anxiety buzz over her skin. "Have you ever seen them together at any other time?"

Ruth shook her head. "Just that night and when the interviews were taking place."

"Did you ask Rosa if she was on a date with Detective Walton?" Juliet asked.

"No." Ruth gave a quick laugh. "I didn't want her to think I was spying on her."

Juliet and Shelly exchanged a look ... each one thinking the same thing. It might be a good idea to talk to Rosa Perkins again.

19

Shelly and Juliet entered the third pub in Paxton Park and finally hit pay dirt. Rosa Perkins sat on the stool next to a high-top table talking with an older man about sports while she enjoyed a glass of wine.

"There she is." Juliet's voice carried a triumphant tone. "I've seen her on some Wednesday nights out with friends. It seems to be a ritual of theirs. I knew we'd find her in one of these bars."

Shelly walked over and greeted Rosa just as the older man was walking away. "How are you? Are you meeting friends?"

"Yeah, I'm supposed to be," the attractive brunette said. "Two girls I've known since high school. The car is giving them trouble. I don't know if they'll make it or not."

"How about we substitute for them for a little while?" Juliet gestured to the chairs around the table asking to join the young woman.

"Oh sure. Have a seat. You can protect me from the men who think a woman alone can't wait to talk to them." Rosa smiled. "I know most people just want to chat, but some ignore the message that I'm not interested in them and then they get testy when I don't fawn over them." Looking down at her glass, she said, "Sort of like Grant was."

"Grant would get angry with you?" Shelly asked.

"I guess you could call it that." Rosa sipped from her drink. "He'd come by my desk sometimes when Shannon wasn't around and flirt with me. I had work to do and didn't want him bothering me. He'd get defensive and annoyed and almost challenging. I didn't like being around him when he got like that. He'd try to blow it off as him only joking. I didn't believe his claim. Grant had an edge to him that wasn't all that attractive."

"Did he finally get the message you weren't interested in him?" Shelly asked.

Rosa said, "He knew I wasn't interested in him, but that didn't stop him from being a pain. It almost made it worse. Like he wanted to bother me because I shot down his advances. Grant could be difficult. My heart would sink when I saw him approaching. I didn't want to deal with him."

"You know the detective?" Juliet asked. "Andrew Walton."

Rosa looked blank for a few seconds and then her face brightened. "Yeah. He was interviewing us at the barn after the crime. You know him, right? He's working on the case, trying to figure out what happened."

"Right," Juliet said. "That's him. I understand you and Detective Walton were outside the barn offices a few nights before the murders."

Rosa blinked a couple of times. "He came by because I called the police station."

Shelly's expression showed surprise. "Did you? What was wrong?"

"I came back to the resort to meet a friend for a late dinner. I park in the barn lot when I come back to go to the pub or one of the restaurants then I walk over to meet my friends. I parked and was going to cut through to the pub by walking past the barn." Rosa sipped from her glass. "I saw someone looking through the windows at the back of the building. It scared me so I hurried back to my car and called the police."

"Why didn't you call resort security?" Juliet asked.

"I didn't even think of it." Rosa's face looked blank.

"What happened after you called?" Shelly asked.

"That detective came by," Rosa said. "He told me he was on his way home when he heard the call. He was close to the resort so he came over to see what was wrong."

"Did he see the person who was looking in the windows?"

"No. When we walked up the walkway, the guy was gone." Rosa looked disappointed.

"You didn't recognize the man?"

"I didn't get a good look at him. His back was to me. His face was pressed against the window," Rosa told them.

"Was there enough light to see anything about him?" Shelly questioned. "His build? His height? Heavy? Skinny? Anything?"

"I told the detective the guy was medium build. He had a hat on so I couldn't see his hair. Something about him made me think he was late twenties or early thirties. Maybe his posture? The way he held himself? Anyway, I didn't see his face."

"What was he wearing?" Shelly asked.

"His hat was pulled down. Probably jeans. Work boots." Rosa's eyes narrowed. "He must have money or his girlfriend does because he was wearing one of those expensive wool jackets. I think it was black. There are wings on the arm patch and on the buttons. You know what brand I'm talking about? I can't think of the name."

"Winter Wings," Juliet said.

"That's it," Rosa smiled. "Super expensive. The guy must have been a resort guest. No one who works there could afford a jacket like that. Unless they saved up for a year."

"What was the guy doing?" Shelly asked.

"He had his face pressed against the window glass," Rosa said. "Why would he be looking into the barn?"

"What room was he looking into?" Shelly asked.

"The back offices." Rosa reached for some peanuts from the bowl in the center of the table.

A shot of adrenaline raced through Shelly's body. "This happened when?"

"A couple of days before the break-in," Rosa said and then her eyes grew wide. "Oh, no. Do you think that was the guy who broke in?" The young woman's hand moved to her throat and she swayed a little on her stool. "Could I have seen the killer?"

"Can you think of anything else about his appearance?" Juliet asked.

"No. I don't think so. I didn't get very close to him."

"What made you call the police? Couldn't he have been a resort worker?" Shelly asked.

"No. He wasn't a resort worker. I'd bet my money on that." Rosa shook her head. "He didn't dress like a resort worker. I got the impression he was probably a visitor."

"Had you ever seen him before or after that night?" Juliet asked.

"I sure don't think so," Rosa said slowly.

"What did Detective Walton say?"

"He didn't say a whole lot. He asked me a million questions. He seemed annoyed that I didn't see the guy leave, that I didn't see which way he went."

"What about footprints?" Shelly asked. "There were probably footprints in the snow?"

Rosa said, "There were footprints in the snow under the window, but you couldn't make out what kind of shoes or boots they were. They were all messed up like he kicked the snow around. There were some vague footprints going from the building to the walkway, but you couldn't tell which way he went because there are a ton of footprints on that walkway. So many people go back and forth there all day long."

"Did the guy remind you of anyone?" Juliet asked.

"Not really. I see a million guys at the resort every day. After a while, they all blend together," Rosa said.

"So he had a medium build?" Shelly asked.

"It seemed like it, but he had on a wool jacket. Without it, he could have been slim."

"But not heavy?"

"Definitely not heavy," Rosa said with confidence.

"Tall?"

"Not short. Definitely on the tall side. Maybe five foot, eleven inches? Maybe six feet?"

"Glasses?"

"I don't know."

"How about facial hair?" Shelly prodded.

"I couldn't really see his face. His back was towards me." With each question she couldn't answer, Rosa's confidence slipped away.

"What about a car?" Juliet asked. "Did you notice a car in the parking lot?"

Again Rosa shook her head. "There were cars in the lot. I don't know if any of them belonged to this guy."

"But you didn't see him come down the walk, go into the lot, and drive away?" Shelly questioned.

"Absolutely not. I would have recognized the jacket." Rosa pushed at her bangs.

"Did he know you saw him looking in the window?" Shelly asked.

Rosa's breath caught in her throat. "I don't know," she said in a whisper. Leaning closer, she asked with a shaky voice, "If he saw me, do you think I'm in danger?"

A flutter of nervousness danced around in Shelly's stomach. "He probably didn't notice you." While she said the words, Shelly wondered if Rosa's reflection might have shown in the window. "Like you said, lots of people walk along that sidewalk."

Rosa stared at Shelly. "Not at that time of evening. I was the only one."

"Did anything about him seem familiar to you?" Juliet asked.

Rosa's head tilted to the side as she thought. "He sort of made me think of the detective." She gave a chuckle. "But that would be impossible. He couldn't be in two places at once."

AT LAST, Rosa's friends showed up and after about fifteen minutes, Shelly and Juliet left the pub and headed to their car.

"The man at the window reminded Rosa of Andrew Walton, huh?" Shelly narrowed her eyes at her friend.

"She said he couldn't be in two places at the same time," Juliet said.

"That's right, he couldn't be. But he could have been at the window, noticed someone coming up the hill from the parking lot, and when she turned back towards the lot, he took off," Shelly said. "He wasn't in two places. Suppose Detective Walton was at the window, left when Rosa came by, then went to his car, drove around, heard the police call and decided to go back to meet Rosa."

"Oh, no," Juliet almost shouted. "He wanted to talk to Rosa to figure out what she saw so he hustled back to the barn. He needed to figure out if he was safe or not."

"It probably wasn't Andrew Walton at the

window," Shelly suggested. "But it might have been someone who resembles Andrew in some way."

Juliet sighed. "Whoever it was, he must have been casing the place. Preparing to break-in. Getting a good look around before the actual robbery was set in motion. I really hope it wasn't Andrew."

"If only there had been security cameras facing the back of the building," Shelly said with a dejected tone.

If only.

20

Shelly stood in the hallway of the police station waiting outside of Jay's office when the door opened and Andrew Walton and Jay emerged.

"I'll be right back, Shelly," Jay said as she hurried away carrying a folder. "Have a seat in my office."

Andrew paused to talk to the young woman. "How are things going?"

"Slow on my end." Shelly gave the detective a disheartened look.

"It's not so great here either." Andrew leaned against the wall. "It's like wading through molasses trying to make any connections. Everything is coming up empty."

"Things have to turn around soon." Shelly forced a smile.

"When I came here I naively thought there would be little crime in a resort town and anything that came up would be solved quickly," Andrew said and grunted. "How wrong you can be."

"There are a lot of people who come and go here," Shelly said. "Tourists, adventure-seekers, the winter and summer sports enthusiasts. We've got the townspeople, the rural citizens, even some survival-ists and preppers on the other side of the mountain. There are a lot of different people who make the area their home and a lot of different people who come here temporarily. It's really kind of a night-mare scenario for law enforcement."

The corners of Andrew's mouth turned up. "I should have talked to you before I accepted the job in Paxton Park."

"I heard you talked to Rosa Perkins recently," Shelly said.

Andrew's face was blank until realization dawned on him. "Oh, yeah. Rosa Perkins. Dark hair. In her mid-twenties? Works at the barn in the front office." He nodded. "I interviewed her. Didn't you talk to her, too?"

"I did. I'm referring to a few nights before the

murders. She called in about a possible intruder outside the barn."

Andrew stood straight and glanced into Jay's office. "Want to sit? My back is giving me trouble."

The two took chairs in front of Jay's desk with Andrew facing the entryway.

Shelly said, "Rosa used the barn's lot to park in. She was meeting a friend at one of the resort restaurants. You met her in the parking lot to investigate her call."

"That's right. She reported seeing a man peering into the barn's offices through the windows at the back of the place."

"Did you see him?"

Andrew shook his head. "He was gone. If he was ever there at all."

Shelly's eyebrow raised. "You think Rosa was mistaken?"

"Who knows? It was dark, lots of shadows. There aren't a lot of lights along that section of the walkway and at that time of night, there would be hardly anyone around there."

"So you think all she saw was a shadow? What about footprints?"

"There were a ton of footprints in the snow," Andrew said. "The workers move around there all day long. People walk on those sidewalks all day long."

"Were there footprints near the building? Below the window?"

Andrew said, "There were hints of footprints around that spot, but they could have been there earlier. There wasn't anything to go on. Maybe some tourist walked by, wondered what the building was, looked in the windows, and left. A nosy, but innocent action. The woman spotted him and panicked."

"It doesn't sound like she panicked," Shelly said. "But she was concerned someone might be about to break into the building and did the right thing by calling the police." Shelly kept her eyes on Andrew's face. "How come a detective answered a call like that?"

A look of annoyance or something else moved fleetingly over Andrew's face. "I was in the area, driving by. I heard the call and offered to take it. I figured it would take all of fifteen minutes."

"And then the break-in occurred two days later," Shelly pointed out. "Do you think the two events were related?"

"It seems unlikely," Andrew said.

"Why does it?"

"Would a potential robber be so obvious? Would

someone plotting to steal a safe be hanging around at that time of evening? It would be smarter to do reconnaissance late at night. Come at 2am. Pretty sure there would be limited chance to run into someone behind the barn at that time of night."

"Maybe the robber ... and murderer ... isn't very smart," Shelly said. She had the idea that Andrew wasn't taking the matter seriously enough.

"Maybe." Andrew let out a breath. "Listen. Calls come in all the time. Ninety-nine percent of them are false alarms."

"Rosa told me the guy was wearing a very expensive jacket," Shelly said.

"She told me that." Andrew gave a nod. "There are plenty of wealthy guys at the resort. Take a walk-through the lodge. Count up how many people are wearing expensive jackets." The detective was pointing out to Shelly that someone wearing an expensive jacket at a popular ski resort was not a great clue and led to basically nothing.

"I know what you're getting at. At a place like this, an expensive jacket is a dime a dozen. Still, it's something," Shelly said. "Were there any other clues to the person's identity?"

"Nothing. A big fat zero." Andrew sighed. "I can't agree that anyone was even there that night."

"I asked Rosa if the man seemed familiar in any way," Shelly said. "She told me the person's build and movements resembled someone she'd recently met."

The detective cocked his head. "Who did she mean?"

"You," Shelly said.

Not many people would have noticed, but Shelly spotted a muscle twitch at the edge of Andrew's jaw.

"MOST OF THE TIME, Andrew is as cool as a cucumber," Shelly told Juliet as they sat in front of the fire on Shelly's comfortable sofa with Justice curled up in between them. "But his jaw tightened when I told him Rosa said the person peering in the barn windows looked like him."

"Did he deny it?" Juliet asked. "Did he look shocked that someone would say something so unexpected?"

"I wouldn't say shock was the reaction he had. For a second, he seemed almost horrified or frightened or like he wanted to run away. He told me his average appearance would match quite a lot of men in town."

Juliet faced her friend, her eyes wide and disbelieving. "Really? Well, maybe from the back he looks average, but certainly not from the front. Andrew Walton is a very good-looking man."

"You'd better rein in your attraction to him," Shelly cautioned. "I'm getting vibes of worry over Andrew."

"Oh, no." Juliet slumped back against the sofa back. "I sure didn't want to hear that."

"Aren't you slightly suspicious of him?" Shelly asked.

Juliet exhaled loudly. "I'd hoped I was imagining things. Do you think Andrew is involved in the crime at the barn?"

"I don't think our feelings should be dismissed. Something's been picking at me about him. I don't know what the reason is. Andrew is probably completely innocent of any wrong-doing, but I'm suspicious of everyone right now. I suppose I'm being overly-sensitive about all of it. Still...." Shelly let her voice trail off.

"I think we need to keep our eyes open," Juliet said with a disappointed tone to her voice. "We need to keep our eyes on Andrew."

"Which isn't hard to do since he's so good-looking," Shelly joked.

Juliet gave her friend a poke in the arm. "I'll have to overlook his appearance and stay focused on any clues that surface ... unfortunately."

Shelly reached for her laptop on the coffee table.

"What are you doing?" Juliet sipped from her tea mug.

"Let's do some internet sleuthing." Shelly began to tap at the keyboard. "Let's look up Andrew Walton."

Juliet lifted Justice onto her lap and wiggled over the sofa cushions to better see the screen.

Shelly began to read what she'd found on Andrew, his education and training, his time with the Boston police, an article introducing the man who had just joined the Paxton Park police force. A few articles which listed Andrew's placement in road races and skiing events. Announcements highlighting his graduation from high school and his graduation from college. "Nothing of note," Shelly said. "He looks squeaky clean. A guy from an average background who was an academic standout and very athletic."

"No strings of robberies attributed to him wherever he moved to?" Juliet asked. "Not a serial killer?"

"Not yet anyway." Tapping again at the screen, Shelly couldn't help a smile forming over her lips at her friend's comments. Reading another article, she stopped. "Oh."

Justice and Juliet sat up at the same time and stared at Shelly.

"What? You found something bad about him?" Juliet asked.

"Not bad. Sad. Andrew was first on the scene at a bridge accident in Boston. A vehicle going at high speed crashed into the bridge barrier, flipped into the air, and came down on the barrier. The car hung there teetering before falling off the bridge and crashing into the water below. Andrew had rushed to the vehicle with a tool that could break in the windows. There was a little girl in the backseat screaming for him to help." Shelly's voice went hoarse. "Just as he reached it, the car fell. The driver and the little girl were killed."

Juliet stared at the screen with her hand on her heart.

Shelly said softly, "A man had stolen the car with the girl in the back of it."

"How awful. The poor child," Juliet said just as Justice let out a deep hiss.

"Andrew took a leave of absence after the incident," Shelly reported.

"Poor Andrew," Juliet said sadly. "That accident must haunt him."

Shelly stiffened.

Juliet knew the Boston vehicular tragedy that killed her sister haunted Shelly as well. Justice gently rubbed her head against her owner's leg as Juliet put her arm around her friend and pulled her close.

21

A fire crackled in the fireplace, candles flickered on the table, and the aroma of chicken parmesan floated on the air.

"I had a dream last night." Shelly rested her fork on her plate and looked across the table at Jay and Juliet.

Jay's husband was out of town for work and their son was away at college so Shelly invited her and Juliet to come for dinner. Working sixteen hour days, Jay needed a break, but she didn't want to go to a restaurant ... too many questions from curious tourists and concerned townsfolk. Exhausted, she couldn't bear putting on her helpful, patient, reassuring face so the invitation from Shelly was most welcome.

Justice sat on the rocker in the corner of the room listening to the conversation.

"What sort of dream?" Jay asked the young woman.

"The same one as I've had before." Shelly rubbed at her temple. "I'm in a gigantic parking lot. All of the cars parked there look alike. I'm wandering up and down the aisles looking for the right car."

"Are you panicked in the dream?" Juliet asked.

"I feel anxious and I get more frantic the longer the search goes on." Reliving the nightmare made Shelly's stomach clench.

"What happens?" Jay asked. "Do you find the car you're looking for?"

"I'm about to give up. I'm about to fall to my knees when I look up and see a black metal lunch box sitting on the roofs of two cars. I get closer so I can inspect the lunch boxes. I know when I choose the right box, I'll have found the car I'm looking for. I also know if I choose the wrong one, everything is over."

"Do you choose the right one?" Juliet leaned forward, anxious to hear the end of the dream.

"I can't figure out which lunch box is the one I want. I'm about to sob when I hear a sound from behind me. I spin around. Lauren is standing a few yards away. I try to run to her, but I'm stuck in my spot. I can't move." Shelly paused and cleared her throat.

"What happens next?" Jay gently encouraged her to go on with the story.

Looking up, Shelly swallowed. "Lauren smiles at me. All my fear and worry wash away. I feel calm. I know I'll make the right choice. Lauren looks towards one of the cars and I try to follow her gaze, but I'm not sure which one she's looking at. I walk to the car on the right. The lunchbox pops open and I strain to see what's inside, but before I can make it out, the engine starts and the driver's side door opens for me. I look back to Lauren. She holds her hand over her heart and disappears." Shelly wiped at her eyes and whispered, "I always hate it when she leaves me."

"You figured it out," Juliet said softly. "It's a good omen. You were able to find the right lunchbox and the right car."

"Only because Lauren gave me confidence," Shelly said. "I was lost without her."

"What do you think the dream means?" Jay asked.

Shelly breathed deeply and let it out again.

"Things may not be what they seem. Choose carefully ... or else. What isn't what it seems in this case?"

"That is yet to be determined," Juliet said.

"Does the dream ever point you to a suspect or to someone who has done something wrong?" Jay questioned.

"No, never." Shelly's shoulders drooped and then she looked to Jay. "Grant's wife said the lunchbox we returned to her didn't belong to Grant. Did you find a second one at the barn? Did you find Grant's lunch container?"

Jay shook her head slowly. "The one I gave you to return to Grant's wife is the only one we've found."

"Maybe Grant's wife is mistaken?" Juliet asked.

"I don't think so," Jay said. "When I went to see her, she was adamant about it. The one we have does not belong to Grant."

"What do you make of it?" Shelly asked. "The one we found in the barn's refrigerator isn't a new lunchbox. Grant didn't go out and buy a new lunch container to replace his old one. This one looks used. So whose is it? Are there fingerprints on it?"

Jay nodded. "Yes, but only one person's prints are on it."

Juliet's eyes went wide. "Whose are they?"

Jay looked from Juliet to Shelly. "Grant's."

Shelly blinked, not understanding, and then her eyes narrowed. "Only Grant's? That's not possible. His wife made his lunch. Why weren't her prints on the box? Someone from the barn probably touched the lunchbox to move it out of the way on the refrigerator shelf. There can't be only one set of prints on that box."

"Exactly," Jay said.

"Did someone plant Grant's fingerprints on the lunchbox?" Juliet asked.

Justice stood up and hissed.

"Why would someone do that?" Shelly asked, her forehead scrunched in thought.

Jay's mouth turned down into a frown and one of her shoulders shrugged. "Your guess is as good as mine. We don't know. Maybe somehow other prints were innocently wiped off?"

"Isn't that unlikely?" Shelly asked.

"In this case, who knows?" Jay reached for her wine and took a long swallow. "Want to talk about something else for a while? I'm just about worn out."

AFTER DINNER WAS FINISHED, Jay thanked Shelly for

her hospitality and, with a yawn, said goodnight, needing to head home to crawl into bed. Juliet suggested to Shelly they go out to one of the resort's restaurant-pubs to meet a few friends for an hour or two so they filled the dishwasher, gave Justice a pat on the head, and drove the short distance to the resort.

Several of the young women's coworkers and their friends gathered at the end of the bar near the large windows that looked out onto the lighted mountain slopes where skiers were enjoying the last runs of the night. Upbeat music played, and the group chatted and laughed together.

Two men standing near the bar were talking and caught Shelly's attention when one of them said, "I can't believe that guy is a cop here in town now."

"Yeah. Standards must be low these days if they accepted him to the police academy."

Shelly slid closer to the men and gave them a smile. "Who do you mean?"

The first young man eyed her and she didn't think he was going to answer, when he seemed to change his mind. "That new cop. Walton. He's been working in town for about six months."

"Do you know him? Why did you say you can't believe he works here?"

"It's not him working here that surprises me," the man said. "It's that he's a cop."

"You don't think he makes a good officer?" Shelly asked.

The second guy snorted. "Walton must have pulled the wool over everyone's eyes to become a police officer. It's like the fox guarding the hen house."

"Really? Why?" Shelly wanted to hear more.

The first man's face hardened. "Walton was a real piece of work years ago. He dated my sister. He beat her up one night."

Shelly's heart began to race. "He did? Did he get arrested?"

"He did not. His father was a big cheese in our town. Walton got off. My sister got a broken nose."

"Was Walton trouble? Did he get into trouble a lot?" Shelly asked.

"He did plenty wrong, but nothing ever stuck to him. It burned me up."

"Maybe Walton turned himself around," Shelly suggested. "Maybe he matured and decided to do things right."

"No. Impossible," the man told her.

The second man said, "I heard he sold drugs back then."

"He ran a drug ring is what I heard. He's probably still doing it."

"Do you think some of the talk about Walton might have been idle gossip?" Shelly asked.

The man who said his sister was hurt by Walton spoke. "It wasn't gossip. It was fact. Walton could be volatile. He had a temper. He was vengeful. No one wanted to cross him."

"Do you know Walton's cousin? Detective Andrew Walton? He works here in town, too."

The two guys exchanged a look.

"Maybe that's how Porter got the job here. His cousin must have helped him."

Juliet sidled up to her friend. "Look who came into the restaurant."

Shelly followed Juliet's eyes to see Troy Broadmoor standing at the hostess station.

"You see what he's wearing?" Juliet asked.

Shelly stared across the room. "Is it one of those expensive jackets?"

"It sure is." Juliet turned to her friend and raised an eyebrow. "How about we go over there and say hello."

When the friends approached Troy and greeted him, he turned around nervously. "Oh, hi." The man was pale and looked thinner than he had when they last saw him.

"How are you?" Juliet asked.

"I'm picking up some take-out dinners." He glanced around the pub-restaurant, his eyes flicking quickly from person to person. "I'm still uncomfortable around people I don't know. I'm getting better, but.... My wife is in the car. She's been working with me to help me overcome my anxiety. She sends me in alone so I can practice." Troy looked sheepish. "Little steps."

"That's right." Shelly gave the man an encouraging smile. "Small things first."

"That's a very nice jacket you're wearing," Juliet said, admiring the Winter Wings garment.

"Oh, thanks." Troy pushed his hands into his pockets. "It was my brother-in-law's jacket. He got something new and passed it on to me. We're the same size." He hurriedly added, "I could never afford to buy it myself."

"Well, it's beautiful. It looks brand new," Juliet said. "You're lucky. I'd love one of those jackets."

The hostess came up to her station carrying Troy's take-out boxes and rang up the order.

"Nice to see you." Troy turned to pay for the meals.

As they were walking back to their friends, Juliet whispered. "Did you notice the same thing I did?"

"Yes," Shelly said. "Troy's expensive coat is missing two buttons."

"And from the back," Juliet said, "he could be mistaken for Andrew Walton."

22

Shelly and Jack had spent the early evening hiking over the lighted mountain trails. It had been peaceful and quiet in the hushed forest with the cold temperatures keeping most people away from the winding paths. Sitting by the restaurant windows enjoying dinner together, the silver moon sat high in the inky sky in contrast to the shadows of the tall pines reaching over the snow.

Jack and Shelly kept the conversation away from the crime and instead, talked about the upcoming winter carnival's craft beer and food festival.

"It's a lot of fun," Jack explained to his girlfriend who was experiencing her first winter living in Paxton Park. "There are food and beer stalls set up all over the area around the pond. There's skating and a huge bonfire. Later in the evening, there are fireworks. We need to go. You'll love it. Let's get Juliet and some other friends to meet up there."

"I'd love to go. Juliet's been telling me how fun it is." Shelly lifted a forkful of the chocolate torte to her mouth. "This is delicious. I think it has more calories than we burned off on the hike."

"After we finish eating, we'd better go back and hike some more," Jack kidded.

Shelly's chuckle tinkled like little brass bells.

"Look over by the fireplace. There's Shannon Flay and that new guy, Finny, from the barn," Jack said.

Shelly let out a soft groan. "I hope they don't come over here. I don't want to talk about the murders tonight."

"Too late," Jack told her. "Here they come."

Shelly watched them out the corner of her eye. "It looks like Shannon doesn't want to come over here. Finny seemed to need to convince her."

"Hey," Finny used a friendly tone as he and Shannon approached.

Looking up like she had no idea the couple was in the restaurant, Shelly said, "Oh, hi."

Jack, who knew both of them superficially, stood up and shook hands with Finny and Shannon. Finny wore a pair of black slacks and a neatly-ironed pale blue, long-sleeved shirt while Shannon had on high heels and a skin-tight coral-colored dress, was wearing a good amount of makeup, and wore her curled hair in a long ponytail that draped over her shoulder. Shelly thought she looked like a celebrity and could see why men flocked to her.

"Are you finishing dinner?" Finny asked. "Do you mind if we join you? We were just going to order coffee and dessert."

Reluctantly, Shelly gestured to the two empty seats around the table and the foursome engaged in small talk. Wondering why Finny and Shannon would want to sit with them instead of enjoying their date alone, Shelly kept an eye on their facial expressions. Clearly, it was only Finny who had wanted to join them.

"Listen," Finny leaned forward. "I've been thinking about Grant."

"What have you been thinking?" Shelly asked as slight annoyance flicked through her at being drawn into a discussion about the murders.

Finny took a quick look at Shannon. "Do you want to tell them?"

"No. You tell them." She flashed her eyes at the

young man and smoothed her skirt. "I'm not the one who thinks it's important."

Finny shrugged a shoulder at Shannon's disinterest. "I figure we can tell you and then you can decide if it's something you should pass on to the police."

"It's really not a big deal," Shannon rolled her eyes.

"Anyway," Finny said, "Grant knew Porter Walton back in high school."

Shannon sighed. "If she's been doing interviews for the police, she must know this already."

Finny looked at Shelly.

"I believe that's right," Shelly said. "There's a regional high school. Kids from different towns attend there. I think Grant and Porter went there."

"Well, I hear from people the two guys didn't get along," Finny said. "I've seen them a couple of times. Once in a bar ... I think I told you this already. The police were called because Grant was being a pain. Porter showed up and made Grant leave. Grant was not happy about that."

"Where was the second time you saw them?" Shelly asked.

Finny ran his hand over the top of his head and once again took a glance at Shannon. "I came to work really early one morning. It was around 4:30am. I had the odd feeling I'd left a gas can behind the wheel of one of the snow removal vehicles. I tossed and turned until I couldn't stand it anymore. I was afraid somebody would run over the can and it would blow up. It's stupid, I know, but the idea wouldn't leave my head so I got up and went into work. It was dark. I walked up the sidewalk from the parking lot to head over to the garages behind the barn."

Nervous tension caused Shelly's neck muscles to ache. "Did you see something?"

"I didn't see anything. I heard voices. They sounded angry."

"Where were the voices coming from?" Shelly asked.

"Around the back of the first garage building," Finny said and then looked over his shoulders to be sure no one was coming close to them. "It was Grant and a guy talking. They didn't seem to be getting along. I stood close to the side of the building. I wanted to hear what they were saying. It was unusual for Grant to be at work so early. No one else was around."

"Except the guy who was talking to Grant," Jack pointed out.

"Yeah. It was that cop. Porter Walton." Finny said.

"Could you hear what they were talking about?" Shelly asked.

"Only a little. The cop was mad. He told Grant he'd better back down. Walton told Grant he wasn't going to get into trouble because of him. He said something about the past, but I couldn't make it out."

"Did Grant speak loud enough that you could hear what *he* was saying?" Shelly asked.

"He said something like Walton was no good back then and he was no good now. Something like that."

"Did the argument go on for a while? How did it end?" Shelly asked.

"I took off. I didn't like the sound of the whole thing. It made me nervous." Finny fiddled with the end of his shirt sleeve. "So I don't know how it ended."

"When did this take place?" Jack questioned. "When did you see them arguing?"

"A couple of mornings before Grant and Benny got murdered." Finny's face was tight and pinched.

"Did you tell this information to the police?" Shelly asked.

Finny shook his head. "Nah. You can tell them, if you want, but I'm not going to the police station myself."

"Why don't you want to report this yourself?"

"I told you before ... I don't like cops. I don't trust them. I'm new at the barn. Wouldn't it be easy to pin those murders on me?"

"There isn't any evidence against you," Jack pointed out. "The crime can't be pinned on you."

Finny's eyes flicked nervously around the room. "I didn't like Grant, but I didn't do anything to either one of those guys." The dark-haired man looked to the attractive young woman sitting beside him. "Shannon wants to tell you something, too."

Shannon gave Finny a look that could kill and then she turned to Shelly. "I really don't have anything to say. Finny and I were just talking. I don't want to say anything bad about anyone."

"Do you think you might know something about what happened at the barn?" Shelly asked the woman with a kind voice.

Shannon's fingers ran through the ends of her ponytail. "I don't know anything."

The waiter cleared some dishes from the table and then poured coffee for everyone. Shelly stifled a sigh. She'd wanted to spend the evening in Jack's company and wished that if Shannon had something to share, she would get on with it.

"Tell them what you think Grant said," Finny encouraged. "Tell them what you think he was talking about."

Daggers flew from Shannon's eyes. "I don't want to spread rumors."

"You heard him so it's not a rumor," Finny explained.

Shannon's lips were tight and thin when she raised her eyes to Shelly. "I was at the barn. I was working a little later than usual. I was going towards the kitchen when I heard Grant's voice. He was talking on the phone."

"He was talking in a whisper," Finny added to the story.

Shannon gave him a look. "Grant was talking in a soft voice. He didn't know I was around. He was standing in the mechanic's office with the lights off."

"What was he saying?" Shelly asked when Shannon seemed like she wasn't going to say any more.

Shannon shifted her eyes downward. "I heard him say *it's payback time. I've got him good and now it's time for him to pay.*"

A cold shiver moved over Shelly's skin. "Do you know who Grant was talking to?"

"No. No idea." Shannon took a long sip of her hot coffee.

"When did you hear Grant say this?" Shelly asked.

Shannon moved around on her seat. "I don't remember exactly. It was probably the week before he died."

"Do you have an inkling what Grant might have been referring to?" Shelly asked.

"I don't know what he was talking about or who he was talking to." Shannon shook her head.

"Do you think Grant had a hand in the attempted robbery of the safe?" Jack asked.

"Was he that stupid?" Shannon asked with an exasperated tone. "Did Grant think he could steal that safe? Did he try to?" The woman moaned. "Really? Grant knew the safe was cemented into the office floor. How could he be so stupid to help someone steal it?"

"What about Benny?" Jack asked. "Would Benny go along with something illegal? Would Benny go along with whatever Grant asked of him?"

Shannon straightened in her seat. "No. Benny wasn't stupid. He wouldn't do anything like that. He wouldn't have helped Grant with something like that."

"If Grant had something to do with the robbery, do you think he could have killed Benny?" Shelly asked. "Would he do that to a friend?"

Shannon looked a little pale under all of her makeup. "I don't think Grant would hurt Benny. But maybe the person Grant was working with would."

23

—————

As Juliet maneuvered the car over the narrow country road, Shelly gripped the arm of the door and tried to control her breathing by slowly taking a breath in and then slowly letting it out.

"Are you okay?" Juliet took a quick glance at her friend knowing she suffered distress while riding in a vehicle.

"I'm fine." Little beads of perspiration showed on Shelly's forehead. "We're almost there."

Juliet pulled into the lot of a little country store and cut the engine. "I thought we should talk before we get to Emmy Norris's house. It's less than five minutes away. If we stop for a few minutes, it will give you a chance to collect yourself."

Shelly gave a grateful nod.

The young women had made arrangements to speak with Grant's wife, Emmy, again.

Juliet said, "I've been feeling sorry for Emmy. Her husband dead, money worries. It would be hard not to feel bad for Emmy's predicament. But ... I don't trust her. Melody from the diner told you Emmy stole from her own mother. She didn't seem all that heartbroken over Grant except that she wouldn't have his income to help with the finances anymore."

Shelly used a tissue to dab at her forehead. "I've been thinking the same thing. It was hard to read Emmy the first time I was there. One second, I was so sad for her, and the next, I thought she was hard and uncaring. I also think we can't believe what comes out of her mouth."

"This interview might be a time to heed the warning in your dreams," Juliet said.

Shelly nodded and put the passenger side window down to get some air. "Some things aren't what they seem. We need to question everything. I've been going over everything that Finny and Shannon said last night. Are they trying to make us believe Grant was in on the robbery? Are they trying to turn attention away from someone else?"

"Like themselves?" Juliet asked. "Finny and

Shannon might be the ones who planned and executed the crime. They might push the idea Grant was in on it to move suspicion from themselves. They were also pushing the idea that Grant and Porter Walton have issues."

"Are Finny and Shannon being honest? Is something going on between Grant and Porter?" Shelly asked. "Or are Shannon and Finny playing us and making things up about the men to make us suspect them of wrongdoing?"

"We need to be on our toes when we talk to Emmy," Juliet said and started the engine. "Hang tight. We'll be at the house in a few minutes."

"What's wrong with the police?" Emmy asked with an edge to her voice. "I didn't really care if I got Grant's lunchbox back, but now I want it. How could they lose it?"

The three women sat in the living room of the small cottage with cups of tea. The place was a mess with clothes flung over the back of chairs, a couple of dirty plates on the coffee table, dirty slush marks on the carpet. A stale odor of cigarettes and old takeout pizza lingered on the air and caused a wave of nausea to squeeze Shelly's stomach.

"I don't know if the police have found your husband's lunchbox. Somehow the one they have was mistaken for Grant's," Shelly said. "Do you know if someone at the barn had a similar looking lunchbox?"

A flash of annoyance passed over the woman's face. "How would I know? I only know the one you brought here the other day doesn't belong to Grant … and I want to know where Grant's box is." Emmy's hair hung in strands around her face giving the appearance of not having been washed in days. Dark half-circles showed on the skin below her eyes. She held an unlit cigarette between the fingers of her right hand and used it to poke the air for emphasis when she talked.

"The police are working on it," Juliet said in a comforting tone of voice.

"Could you tell us how Grant was feeling prior to the day he was killed?" Shelly asked.

Emmy gave her a dirty look. "We've been over and over this."

"It helps to go over things more than once." Shelly gave the woman a slight smile.

Emmy pushed her stringy bangs from her forehead. "What was the question?"

"How was Grant's mood? Did he seem like himself?" Shelly repeated.

"He was fine."

"Was he happy at work?" Juliet asked.

Emmy looked up. "He was the same as always."

Shelly asked, "Was he looking forward to anything? Did the two of you have plans for anything?"

Emmy looked stone-faced. "No."

"Have you been working, Emmy?" Juliet asked. "Have you been able to return to work?"

"Some, yeah. I need the money to move. I'm going to live with my sister in New Jersey for a while. My sister was supposed to come up here and help me, but she couldn't get the time off from work." The woman put her head in her hands. "Stupid, Grant," she whispered.

"Why do you say that?" Shelly asked.

Emmy sat up. "He always had a scheme. Was always into something. Nothing ever worked out."

"Did Grant have a scheme going on recently?" Shelly asked.

"What?" Emmy shook her head. "No."

"Was he trying to make a little extra money?" Juliet questioned.

"He was always trying to make some extra money." Emmy blew out a breath.

"How did he try to make money?" Juliet lifted her mug from the coffee table.

"Selling stuff, fixing things up, stuff like that." Emmy's voice betrayed the woman's exhaustion.

"Who was Grant friendly with?" Juliet asked before taking a sip of her coffee.

"Benny. You mean at work or outside of work?" Emmy held her hands together in her lap.

"Either."

"He had a few guys he hung out with. He knew them from high school. They'd go out for a beer, play darts, go fishing, get together to watch sports."

"He was still friends with people from high school?" Shelly asked. "That's great."

"Yeah, he was." Emmy rubbed at her forehead.

"The new officer from town went to Grant's high school. He came to talk to you the first time Shelly came here," Juliet said in a light voice. "Grant must have known him. Porter Walton. Did Grant ever talk about Porter?"

Emmy's head snapped to attention. "Once in a while. Not much."

"Had they gotten together since Porter moved here?" Juliet questioned.

"No. They weren't close in high school," Emmy said.

"Had Grant run into Porter in town?" Shelly asked.

Emmy flicked her eyes to Shelly. "I don't think so. Grant didn't tell me he'd run into him."

"Someone told us that Porter had to bounce Grant from a bar not long ago," Juliet said.

Emmy's eyebrows shot up. "I didn't know that."

"Grant didn't mention it to you?" Shelly reached for her mug.

"I don't think so. I don't remember anything about it."

"Someone at the barn heard Grant on the phone with someone," Juliet said. "He was talking to someone about payback. It happened right before the murders took place."

Emmy sucked in a breath.

"Do you know what Grant meant by *payback*?" Shelly asked. "Do you know who he might have been talking with?"

Emmy reached up to fiddle with a strand of her white-blond hair. "Payback? What does that mean? Why would Grant say that?"

"We wondered the same thing," Juliet said.

"I don't know," Emmy said again and then noticed Shelly's cup was empty. "Do you want more tea?"

"Yes, please. That would be nice."

Emmy's hand shook as she reached for the mug on the table.

Noticing the woman's trembling hand, Shelly said, "I can get it, if you like."

"Okay," Emmy said weakly. "The teabags are in the closet in the kitchen. The water in the pot should still be hot."

After asking if Emmy or Juliet wanted a second cup, Shelly headed down the dark hall to the kitchen at the back of the house. She rinsed her cup in the sink and then opened the closet to find the box of teabags. As she took it from the shelf, she noticed a handbag with a price tag still on it sitting on the upper shelf.

Glancing down the hall and hearing the two women talking in the living room, Shelly reached for the bag and brought it down off the shelf. A Louis Vuitton. She almost gasped when she saw the price. Hurrying to put it back, Shelly noticed several boxes stacked on top of each other. She took one down. Inside was a leather jacket from a well-known

232

designer. Checking the other boxes, she found more expensive things.

After calculating the cost of the items in her head, Shelly realized the merchandise was worth ten thousand dollars.

She put everything back on the top shelf and then as she hurriedly poured herself another cup of tea, she saw a small piece of paper with a list of five names and telephone numbers. When she read one of the names, Shelly's heart skipped a beat ... *Andrew Walton* ... his name and number had been hastily scrawled at the bottom of the paper.

Shelly carried her mug back to the living room where she took her seat. "Sorry it took so long. I heated the water up again." She listened as Juliet asked a few more questions and Emmy answered them.

"Has Detective Walton been in touch with you?" Shelly asked.

Emmy rolled her eyes slightly. "I told you already. Grant wasn't close to Porter Walton in high school. There was no reason he'd get in touch with me. The only time I met him was when he came here with you and that police woman."

"I meant Porter's cousin, Andrew." Shelly watched Emmy's face.

Emmy paused for a second. "Andrew?"

"Porter isn't a detective," Shelly explained. "His cousin Andrew works here in town as a detective."

"Oh," Emmy said.

"Do you know him?" Shelly asked.

"No, I don't think so." Emmy gave her pat answer and pushed at her bangs again.

Shelly wanted to ask another question, but didn't.

Then why do you have his name and number on the pad of paper in the kitchen? Or maybe it was Grant who wrote it there?

Was Andrew Walton in on the robbery and murders?

24

On the way home from Emmy's house, Juliet called Jay to report that the woman had high-end merchandise on the top shelf of her kitchen closet and Andrew's name and number was on a pad of paper in the kitchen.

Jay was on the way back to Paxton Park from a meeting two hours away. She wanted an officer to interview Emmy about the expensive items in her possession and decided to send Porter Walton to see the woman.

Shelly's and Juliet's concerns about Porter and Andrew were tabled to be discussed when Jay returned home. "There could be any number of reasons why Porter and Grant were talking near the equipment garages. And Andrew may have spoken to Emmy about Grant's death and the woman simply wrote his name and contact information down on the pad. There isn't enough to be suspicious of either of the men, but I'll look into it when I get back."

Juliet dropped Shelly off at home before heading to the resort to lead a group meeting in mountain survival techniques.

Justice greeted Shelly at the door and followed her around the house not leaving her side for a moment. After making a fire in the fireplace and cooking dinner, she changed into soft sweat pants and a t-shirt and sat on the sofa with the Calico cat watching the flames and telling Justice about the interview with Emmy.

"I know you don't understand a word I'm saying, Justice, but I need to talk it through so tonight you're my sounding board." Shelly scratched the cat behind the ears. "I'm suspicious of everyone, even Andrew and Porter. I don't feel like the dreams I've had are helping me. I must be overlooking something. But what?"

Justice lifted her head and released a shrill howl that caused Shelly to jump.

"How about a little warning before you do that," Shelly said.

The cat leapt onto the floor and paced in front of the fire while Shelly watched her go back and forth. "I feel like I'm watching a tennis match."

Justice stopped in her tracks and stared at the young woman for several moments, then she darted to the side table in front of the window, pushed the drape back with her paw, and sat there watching the road.

"Are you expecting someone?" Shelly laughed and then caught herself in mid-chuckle, her face becoming serious. Getting up and crossing the room, she bent a little to look outside through the window's frosty glass. The street was empty. Snowflakes fell softly and sparkled as they drifted down in the shaft of golden light from the streetlamp.

Turning away from the window, she told the cat, "It's all quiet outside. You don't need to keep watch."

The cat growled low in her throat just as a car's headlights swept the house as it turned into Shelly's driveway.

Goosebumps formed over the young woman's skin when she heard the car door slam and heavy footprints come up the porch steps. When the doorbell rang, Shelly peered through the door's peephole to see the barn's manager, Troy Broadmoor, standing under the porch light.

When Shelly opened the door, Troy shifted from foot to foot and asked if he could come in.

Shelly hesitated, but when Troy told her he had something important to share, she swung the door wide to admit the man.

"I'm sorry to barge in like this. I need to talk to you." Troy shook the snowflakes from his jacket, removed the coat, and handed it to Shelly.

Troy's face was colorless and his breathing seemed quick and shallow. He looked around the room, but didn't seem to be taking anything in. A sheen of sweat covered his forehead.

Shelly gestured for Troy to take a seat and then she sat on the sofa being careful to sit nearest the side table that had a little drawer in it where Shelly kept a small canister of pepper spray. Justice sat next to her owner, her eyes glued on the visitor.

"It's okay. I don't mind you stopping by. What would you like to talk about?" Shelly wondered if Troy was close to a breakdown and if his wife knew where he was. "Where's Roberta? Does she know you went out?"

"Roberta's fine. She's at home." Troy picked at the cuticle of his index finger.

"What would you like to tell me?" Shelly asked using a kind voice.

Troy lifted his eyes as if he were seeing Shelly for the first time. "I wanted to tell you something. I don't know if I should tell the police."

"Go ahead. It's okay to tell me." Adrenaline coursed through Shelly's veins.

"I saw something," Troy said in a whisper.

Shelly waited for the man to continue.

"I saw something that morning."

"The morning of the robbery?" Shelly asked.

"I was late. I slept late. I know people think I'm lying about that, but it's the honest truth."

Shelly nodded encouragingly.

"I went inside. Shannon was out. She wasn't feeling well. I had an email message from her, but I didn't see it until later." Troy clasped and unclasped his hands. "The place was so quiet. There was something almost eerie about it. It scared me." The man looked at Shelly. "I looked around as I walked back to my office. Something seemed off. I heard something ... maybe like the scuff of a shoe. I turned down the hall and saw the backdoor bang shut. It opened and shut in the wind.

Bang, bang. The latch hadn't caught. I noticed the hallway floor was wet. Something. Something made me hurry to the door. I looked out the small window."

Troy stared at Shelly, blinking.

Justice sat as still as a statue.

"What did you see?" With her heart pounding, Shelly asked the question as softly as she could, not wanting to break Troy out of his story.

"A man. He was running towards the woods."

"Do you know who he was?"

"I could only see his back. He was carrying something in one hand. It was black."

"What was it? Could you see what it was?" Shelly had a pretty good idea what it might have been.

"It looked like a lunchbox."

"What happened next?"

"The wind caught the door again. It swung open and then slammed in my face. The noise of it made me whirl around. My office door was partially closed. When I hurried to the backdoor, I couldn't see inside the office, but from my position near the rear door, I could see. I could see a foot. A shoe. I walked closer." Troy's eyes filled up. "That's when I found them."

Justice released a low growl.

"The person running away from the barn ... did you recognize him?" Shelly asked.

"I didn't. But he had on a jacket like mine. The one I got from my brother-in-law."

"What color was the jacket?"

"Black. It looked black."

"Did the person remind you of anyone?" Shelly asked.

Troy's face looked like it was going to crumple.

"It's okay," Shelly told the man.

"It sort of looked like one of those police officers. You know those two who are related?"

"The Waltons?" Shelly's heart was practically in her throat.

"Yes. Them."

"Have you told anyone this?" Shelly questioned.

"I didn't tell anyone, not even Roberta. I was afraid." Troy leaned forward and whispered. "If it *was* a cop, well, I was afraid of what he might do to me if I said I saw him at the crime scene."

"So I'm the only one you've told this to?"

"Yes. Except I saw Emmy at the store today."

Shelly's stopped breathing for a second. "Emmy? Grant's wife?"

"I told her she'd better look out for those cop cousins." Troy nodded vigorously.

Justice let out a mighty howl and raced to the window.

"Is someone coming?" Troy asked with a touch of fear in his voice.

Shelly went to the window. This time a car parked behind Troy's vehicle and Andrew Walton got out of his car.

Shelly grabbed her jacket. "I'm going outside for a few minutes. Don't come out. Stay here. Stay inside the house. Do you understand, Troy?"

"Yes."

Shelly stepped onto the porch and slammed the door behind her, suspicious of the man who had parked in her driveway. "What are you doing here?" she demanded.

Andrew went around to the back of his car. "I need to talk to you. Jay is out of town. I need to show you something."

Shelly's heart raced. She didn't trust him. "Not now. It isn't a good time."

"Can I come in?" Andrew asked. "Could you keep some things here for me for a little while?"

"No. I'm expecting Jack," Shelly lied. She could hear the cat howling and shrieking inside the house and it sent a shot of fear through her body.

"I'll only take a few seconds. I need to show you

something," Andrew said. "It's important. Can you keep it here for me?" Just as Andrew opened the back door of the car and leaned in to retrieve something from the seat, a car raced down the street with its passenger side window open.

Inside the house, Justice knocked the lamp off the side table causing a mighty crash.

Shelly could see a shadow inside the vehicle and her instinct told her to drop. She fell to the porch as something flashed red and a roar came from the car that screeched to a halt in front of her house.

"Andrew!" Shelly screamed.

Andrew stood up and turned as his cousin, Porter, got of his car and stood next to the driver's side.

"You broke into my house," Porter screeched at Andrew. "Those things don't belong to me. You don't know what you're doing. You're aren't going to pin this on me. You can't prove anything."

On her hands and knees, Shelly peeked through the slats of the porch railing and saw Andrew moving his hand slowly towards his gun.

Porter took aim, but Andrew was faster and he shot his cousin through the open front windows of the man's car.

Porter fell.

As Andrew dashed to him, he yelled to Shelly. "Call 911."

Shelly opened the front door and raced inside to get her phone. She punched the numbers into the phone as she grabbed a blanket and ran back outside.

Justice was already out and standing guard beside Andrew who knelt next to his bleeding cousin, tears streaming down his face. "Porter. Why? Why did you do it?"

Shelly and Andrew used the blanket to try and stay the unconscious man's bleeding and sat together on the snowy sidewalk until the ambulance finally arrived.

25

"Porter will survive his injury," Jay sat behind the old desk in her office giving Shelly and Juliet an update on the case. "Andrew suspected his cousin of wrong doing, but he didn't want to accuse a fellow police officer until he had more evidence. Andrew entered his cousin's apartment, *invited* I might add, and found Grant's lunchbox and the jacket Porter used during the crime. The jacket had a missing button. Grant and Benny must have fought Porter in the office and the button was pulled off in the fight."

"Will the jacket and the lunchbox be admissible in court?" Shelly asked. "Andrew didn't have a search warrant to look for those things."

Jay said, "Porter asked Andrew to pick up his

wallet from the apartment. Andrew entered the bedroom to get the wallet from the dresser. The closet was open and Andrew spotted the lunchbox stuffed in the back behind a bunch of shoes. He didn't have to touch anything to see it. The Winter Wings jacket was in the closet, too. He photographed the closet and removed the items for evidence." Jay continued. "Andrew knew I was away from town for the day. He didn't want to leave the lunchbox and jacket at the police station without first talking to me about them."

"Andrew told me he wanted to drop the things off at Juliet's house, but she wasn't at home," Shelly said. "So he was going to ask me if he could leave the items with me until you arrived home."

"That's right," Jay said. "The jacket's fibers are consistent with those taken from under Grant's fingernails and the lunchbox in Porter's closet belonged to Grant."

"Why take the man's lunchbox?" Juliet asked.

With a sigh, Jay leaned back in her chair. "As you know, Grant and Porter attended the same high school. There was quite a bit of hostility, anger, and resentment between the men. It infuriated Grant that Porter was a police officer. He and Porter had sold drugs together during the last two years of high school. According to his wife, Grant said Porter stole his profits from their business and pushed him out. Porter continued to sell even to this day and reported to us that Grant threatened to expose him as a drug dealer. Porter offered to bring him into the business, but it was a lie. Porter received information about the money in the barn's safe from Grant and promised him half of it for providing details about the easiest and safest time to hit the office. To show good faith, Porter promised to put fifteen thousand dollars into Grant's lunchbox on the morning of the robbery."

"That's how Porter had Grant's lunchbox in his apartment," Juliet said.

"Porter never planned to give Grant half the money because he wasn't going to steal the safe. He made up the whole thing to set up Grant," Jay said. "Porter was sick of him and his threat to expose his drug business. He decided to finish Grant off and to get him out of his life once and for all. Benny was killed because he was with Grant."

"What a terrible mess," Shelly shook her head sadly.

Jay said, "After he killed Grant and Benny, we assume Porter went to the refrigerator, grabbed Grant's lunchbox that he'd put the fifteen thousand dollars in, and replaced it with a similar one ... the thinking being that suspicion would fall on Grant if things were out of the ordinary. Grant brought his lunchbox to work every single day. If Grant was suspected of involvement in the robbery, Porter was sure things would eventually be traced back to him. This is what we've pieced together from talking to Grant's wife, Emmy."

"She obviously knew what Grant was up to," Shelly said. "Emmy was expecting the money from the robbery so she went on a spending spree and bought all that high-end merchandise I found in her kitchen closet."

Jay added, "Emmy told us Grant said it was payback time for Porter for having cheated him out of all those profits in high school. Grant planned to keep up his threats to expose Porter's illegal activities until he'd made plenty of money off the guy. Grant told Emmy he wasn't going to get conned by Porter ever again. Porter threatened Emmy to stay quiet about what she thought had happened or she'd end up just like Grant."

"Grant should have left it alone," Juliet said.

"But if he did, Porter may never have been exposed," Shelly pointed out. "Andrew must be very upset about his cousin."

"He is," Jay said. "Andrew's been through some tough experiences as a law enforcement officer. He's resilient though. He'll make it through this, too. We all need to give him our support."

"Why was Andrew's name and number on the pad at Emmy's house?" Juliet asked.

"Andrew had gone to the house to talk to Emmy again," Jay said. "He questioned her about Grant's and Porter's relationship. He asked her to please contact him if anything came up."

"My dreams didn't help us very much this time," Shelly pondered out loud.

"Yes, they did," Juliet said. "They pointed to things that weren't what they seemed. Porter is exactly what the dreams suggested. He was not what he seemed to be."

"I guess I need to work on interpreting the dreams better," Shelly said.

"This is all new territory for you," Jay said, "and for us. We'll get better at it. I'm grateful for your help."

SHELLY AND JACK snuggled on the sofa watching a movie with a fire crackling in the fireplace and a few candles shimmering on the coffee table. Justice had pushed in between the two people and was now snoozing soundly on her back with her paws in the air.

"This cat makes me want to fall asleep," Jack said smiling down at the feline.

Shelly chuckled. "Justice makes a nap look like the best thing in the whole world."

Jack put his arm around Shelly's shoulders being careful not to squish the cat. "I'm glad this case has been solved. You were a big help to Jay."

"I don't really think I was this time." Shelly held her boyfriend's hand. "Andrew was the one who figured it out. Juliet and I were concerned that Andrew was the killer. I need to learn to pay better attention to things. I need to learn to pull truth from the jumble in my head." With a smile, she said, "I think Justice knew who the killer was all along. She was acting oddly just before Andrew showed up here. Troy told me Justice was going crazy when I went out to the porch. She was howling and trying to climb the drapes. I think she knew Porter was on his way and she knew he was bad."

"I certainly won't deny this cat knows things." Jack reached down and petted the sleeping animal. "I think she's something special." Leaning forward, he gave Shelly a loving kiss. "Just like the woman she lives with."

They watched the movie for another ten minutes and when Shelly swallowed the last of her tea, Jack got up to pour her another cup. As he passed the window that faced the driveway next to Juliet's house, headlights passed over the glass and shone into the room for a moment.

Jack bent a little to look outside.

"Did Juliet come home?" Shelly asked in a sleepy voice.

"Yes, she did." Jack straightened and gave his girlfriend a grin. "You know how you told me earlier that you hoped Andrew was going to be okay?"

Shelly nodded.

"I think he's going to be just fine," Jack said.

"Why do you say that?"

"Because he and Juliet just got out of her car and headed into her house with a pizza." Jack winked. "And they were holding hands."

"Oh." Shelly's eyebrows went up and a wide smile spread over her face as the sweet Calico cat opened one eye and purred her approval.

THANK YOU FOR READING!

To hear about new books and book sales, please sign up for my mailing list at:

www.jawhitingbooks.com

Your email will never be sold, shared, or spammed.

If you enjoyed the book, please consider leaving a review. A few lines are all that's needed. It would be very much appreciated.

ALSO BY J.A. WHITING

OLIVIA MILLER MYSTERIES

SWEET COVE COZY MYSTERIES

LIN COFFIN COZY MYSTERIES

CLAIRE ROLLINS COZY MYSTERIES

PAXTON PARK COZY MYSTERIES

ABOUT THE AUTHOR

J.A. Whiting lives with her family in Massachusetts. Whiting loves reading and writing mystery and suspense stories.

Visit / follow me at:

www.jawhitingbooks.com
www.bookbub.com/authors/j-a-whiting
www.amazon.com/author/jawhiting
www.facebook.com/jawhitingauthor

Made in the USA
Middletown, DE
20 September 2018